PERI ELIZABETH SCOTT

EVERNIGHT PUBLISHING ®

www.evernightpublishing.com

Copyright© 2018

Peri Elizabeth Scott

Editor: Audrey Bobak

Cover Artist: Jay Aheer

ISBN: 978-1-77339-701-6

PERI ELIZABETH SCOTT

DEDICATION

Ruler's Concubine is dedicated to my loyal betas, J.J. Lore and Jennifer Simpkins, wonderful authors in their own right, and to my editor Audrey Bobak, whose considerable expertise made this book shine!

PERI ELIZABETH SCOTT

RULER'S CONCUBINE

Peri Elizabeth Scott

Copyright © 2016

Prologue

"We have done all that can be accomplished, Ruler." The other healer nodded in agreement, and the pity flitting across his stoic face conveyed more than the actual words. Lysett of the House of Daboort inclined his head and schooled his own features, forcing himself to accept the hard, brutal truth. His concubine was dying, and their recently conceived child with her.

It was the same for most unions of his world. Fertile women were few and far between, and those who managed to conceive rarely went full term, the baby always failing to survive if born early. Others, as was now inevitable for his childhood friend, Trosan, succumbed to the pregnancy, long before their child was viable. What should have been an ecstatically happy time for all Meridian couples, learning they were to be parents, was one tainted by fear and anxiety.

It was horrifyingly frustrating, that despite all their renowned technology, the Meridians were unable to address this medical issue. It was thought to be genetic, but if so, the genes mutated with abandon and could not be cataloged or corrected. Post mortems were now allowed, despite the cultural resistance to such things, but each and every case was different. It was time for a change, regardless of the resistance he'd likely face.

"Leave us." He nodded his understanding and appreciation of the fruitless efforts of the healers, despite his lowering heart.

Squaring his shoulders and adopting a calm demeanor, he made his way into the sleeping chamber where he would sit with Trosan until she passed. The symptoms varied from female to female, but they all tended to slip away at the end, oblivious, as their bodies rejected the pregnancy and succumbed to the toxins. Her hand lay passively in his own throughout his vigil, but he told himself she knew he was there as he recounted their childhood adventures together.

"Our union was inevitable, dear friend." He said it out loud to convince himself it was true because had there been another female, one his body and soul responded to, he and Trosan would never have joined. Guilt soaked his being.

"My childhood was full because of you." That rang with utter sincerity, and now his future stretched out emptily.

They were far better friends than lovers. But Trosan was willing to help him accomplish his duty—an heir to carry on the family line. His brother was long dead on the field of battle in a far-off station, and it fell to Lysett to ensure the continuation of his House and its rule.

He smoothed the hair from her brow, marking her pallor. "How am I to rule without you to come home to and soothe my questions and self-doubt? And offer your insight?"

There were some who might disagree, but the majority of Meridia's citizens and those of the outlying planets didn't chafe under his governance, and he did his best to live up to his credo, that of being fair and consistent whilst taking into account cultural differences. It meant a fine line to walk at times, but with Trosan in his home and his parents offering support and counsel despite their advancing years, Lysett couldn't say he regretted his position. Until now. How would he find the time to grieve?

Trosan moved slightly beneath his touch and he held his breath, but she didn't open her eyes, even when he pressed her hand between his. His pain was exacerbated by that terrible guilt and nothing eased it. It had taken his best friend years to conceive, and he secretly wondered if it was because they came together in a lackluster regard for one another sexually, reliant upon the aphrodisiac elixir they imbibed to carry out their joining.

The passionate joinings documented in the tomes of the past had fallen by the wayside in lieu of so-called improvements in lifestyle and far-reaching political aspirations. As Ruler, he was as guilty of perpetuating that lifestyle, perhaps more so.

There were times he also wondered if Trosan longed for a *passionate union* with someone other than himself. Because he struggled from time to time with pressing sexual needs not assuaged by their times together to procreate. He had heated memories of earlier, purely sexual relationships to compare with the one he and Trosan shared, and those now brought him the darkest shame.

He now told himself fiercely he'd take any additional number of years together with only Trosan in his life, forgoing any breeding efforts, if she might live through the affliction.

"I am so sorry, Trosan." He spoke quietly for hours, hoping she heard him and was comforted.

Dawn was breaking in the west when she sighed her last, peaceful breath. It was as if she'd stepped away from him, no stutter in her chest or throat, merely gone. The sense of loss overwhelmed him in that instant, and he fell forward to rest his forehead on her belly, the swell of their child not yet apparent. He murmured his farewell to both, before once again composing himself and moving to the doorway to usher in her parents, inconsolable in their grief.

It was a measure of just how dim the future was for Meridia, with its lack of children, that neither parent displayed any blame toward him for instigating the cause of her death. They accepted their daughter's honorable patriotism and sense of duty, perhaps better than he had.

Feeling adrift, he allowed his own parents to enfold him in their embrace and tried to respond appropriately to their condolences, but all he could think about was how he'd lost his best friend and was still beset with a daunting task. If he didn't produce an heir within the next few years, males of other Houses who'd successfully procreated had the right to seek his office. If it was as simple as that, Lysett might be willing to step aside, and give up rule, but he knew from past history that Meridia would be plunged into civil war as factions battled for supremacy. He refused to be responsible for that if there was another way.

"We both deeply regret your loss, son," his father, Yu'un, said quietly. "We had hoped…"

Ellyce, his mother, wept openly and whispered through her tears. "Trosan has been part of our family for so long. Yes, we had hoped."

He knew the thought of a grandchild had united Trosan's parents again, for they too had married for political reasons, and while they liked and respected one another, love had never fully blossomed. His parents had a grand love, and he believed it significant that both he and his brother had been conceived and carried to term, whereas Trosan was an only child—and a female, the result of considerable medical tinkering. A miracle, she had very nearly not survived her birth—and he'd killed her.

"We all hoped, Mother. Trosan no less than any of us. Duty has taken a terrible toll."

Extricating himself from his mother's hold, he suggested she and Yu'un tend to Trosan's parents and strode down the hall until he reached his work room. Bast was ensconced behind the smaller desk, working diligently on the documents and reports that never seemed to lessen in number, not even when the Ruler's concubine was dying. They both normally worked in the government office, but naturally stayed in his home to be closer to his concubine. The other male jumped to his feet.

"It is over then, Master?" Real sorrow filled Bast's eyes. He'd known Trosan nearly as long as Lysett, and there were times when Lysett thought his first servant's feelings went far deeper for Trosan than he let be known. For a moment, he envied the man his option of immersing himself in the mundane, rather than deal with the sadness of imminent death.

"She is gone, Bast." The statement helped Lysett accept the hard fact with utter intensity and he barely made it to a chair before his legs weakened.

Master and servant sat in silence for some time, the suns rising and spreading their rays and warmth over the thick walls and lilting through narrow windows of Lysett's abode. The shards of light made fanciful patterns on the tile floor and his mind traced over them, searching for a purpose. Finally, he stirred himself.

"It's distasteful to raise the issue, Bast, but duty

waits for nothing and no one. I need an heir. The planet needs one. Have you made any progress?"

Bast's face was strained and his eyes weary, but he immediately turned to the task, taking up a screen tablet from the desk's surface. Tapping through several pages, he nodded in apparent satisfaction, though spoke in an apologetic tone.

"There is no doubt, Master. You are not fated to find a suitable concubine from this world. There are no compatible females in any database. But I have researched Meridia law, Ruler. Extensively. And I have had two of my assistant clerks double-check for me."

Lysett cut his servant off, experiencing no surprise at the news. There had never been a compatible female, other than for casual, if pleasurable, sexual encounters. It was why he and Trosan had mated, and she'd paid the ultimate price. "You're saying I have options. Why is this something we've not heard before?"

With a shrug, Bast set down his screen. "Meridians aren't known for their, uh, acceptance of other cultures. At least they weren't until your House assumed rule. The past speaks for itself. It was all about conquering and acquiring. Things have improved since then, insofar as tolerance levels improving amongst the populace. Perhaps because we lack for nothing else. We could look to other species, and I propose we do so."

Xenophobia had indeed been a historical fact, and Lysett knew that even today old distrusts and elitism remained in a few Houses. Bast was correct in his assumption that none of them would have voluntarily looked outside their own kind for a concubine, not even to bear a child. In truth, Lysett wasn't sure how *he* felt about it, but after losing Trosan, he accepted the fact he likely had no choice. *Meridians* had no choice.

Bast interpreted his silence as condemnation.

"There will be other females from Meridia willing to take the risk, Master, if you believe it is perilous to flout convention. Perhaps with increased medical attention—"

"No, it makes no sense. We have excellent medical knowledge and it would still be sentencing another of our females to death."

"Sir?"

He focused his attention back on his first servant and donned the mantle of his leadership. "I haven't the time. Meridia doesn't have the time. Conception is uncertain and can take so long, and considering the unacceptable probability of the demise of both mother and child … it's time we looked outside our world."

Bast waited patiently, knowing his master well.

Lysett made a snap decision. "Search out any possible candidates from among the other planets. I will leave shortly for the Bra'oor quadrant, to meet with the General of our outpost there."

That particular General was a male after Lysett's own heart, and after hearing Bast's research, he thought to consult with the man about the plan to seek concubines from other species. He wouldn't be overt, but could get a sense of the tolerance for such a thing. As Ruler, Lysett had learned to cloak his plans in distraction, the better to confuse and mislead others who wished him harm. The General had been utterly dependable in the past and would hopefully be so again.

"The Bra'oor aren't candidates, for certain," his first servant offered.

Lysett suppressed a shudder. The pale creatures with their transparent skin and elongated fingers, not to mention the third eyelid, didn't appeal to him at all. He supposed they were elegant and cultured in their own way, but he tended toward…

What exactly *did* draw him? Trosan was tall and

voluptuous, with thick, dark hair that hung in rampant curls over her shoulders like all the other females on his planet, and her eyes were the pale green of their kind. He blocked off the memory and tamped down the misery and loss. He had to attend to his duties, and whomever Bast came up with, her appearance was moot. Perhaps any compatible species would be tougher, and he and his ruling House would be blessed with good fortune. Set the example for his people. He appreciated that other species might not be inclined to mate with a Meridian, but he pushed the vagrant thought aside. The Meridians were conquerors and there were many means to compel victory.

"Find a match, Bast. Goddess willing, you'll be successful." Despite experiencing a sense of betrayal of Trosan, Lysett allowed himself a tiny glimmer of hope that he might yet save his kind.

Chapter One

"Where is she?" The bellow echoed above her and the forest went silent.

Celeste Raynor huddled in the scraggly underbrush, cold and miserable. It was the second time the Searchers had attended her home, and this time, she'd nearly been caught. She hadn't thought they'd come again so soon, and dismissed the early warning alarm as being triggered by one of the large deer who found her garden irresistible. Cobbling together rusting tin cans with painstakingly unwound fishing line might seem a poor means to alert a person, but it worked for her.

The does and their fawns had to be disappointed by the lack of fodder, with only the root vegetables still in the ground, their foliage wilting with the onset of fall. Her garden was the sustenance for her and many of her far-flung neighbors, the same patch of land those idiots had trampled through, sneaking around the back way in an attempt to surprise her. It was the second rattle of tins, tied to a place no herbivore would trespass, that got her outside in time.

"The wench isn't here." The new voice spoke the obvious, but his frustration was apparent. Another crash followed his pronouncement. "Did none of you see a sign?"

Denials sounded faintly and there was an unmistakable snort of derision. "Search again, all nooks and crannies."

She had no idea what the Searchers wanted or why they had been sent to her home, but one didn't hang around and ask questions. All she knew, was that of late, women were snatched up, taken away, and either didn't return home or came back quite different, unable or unwilling to explain what had transpired. She'd heard the rumors and had seen the results with one, and decided not to make it a personal experience.

Slipping out of a side window while two of the Searchers entered through the kitchen door, she had burrowed in behind the bushes that grew close to the old clapboards of the house. Trusting to the subdued colors of her clothing, she lay there motionless, listening to the sounds of the men tromping diligently through each and every room of the ramshackle abode. Loud, harsh voices spilled out of the cracked and badly patched windows, and she heard the unmistakable clatter of things being shoved over and tossed aside. It made her wince, because she had so little, and no way of replacing anything.

"She might be in the village." A whiny tenor voice made the suggestion. "Or at a neighbor's."

Whatever the response was, she couldn't hear it, as they vacated the room over her head. She prayed they didn't decide to search the grounds, but no one came outside to look around, and after an eternity, heavy boots stomped down the warped floorboards on the steps, announcing the Searchers' departure.

She counted up the footsteps, marking the number of men, and her heart sank when she realized they'd left one of their kind back, presumably to wait and watch for her. Idly wondering how he would communicate with the rest if he was lucky enough to catch her—the inhabitants of planet had no devices to perform that task any longer, not since the arrival and departure of the Meridians—she swallowed down a harsh bite of laughter. One better fed, trained, and muscular Searcher against one short, untrained, and hungry woman … he didn't need to call for backup.

Waiting until the light faded demanded considerable, bone-chilling patience, but she schooled herself into subjugating the urge to jump up and run, knowing she wouldn't get past the yard site if he spied her. At least she was on the side of the house closest to the forest, so could lose herself in amongst the trees, once it was dark. She'd face tonight and possibly tomorrow without food or shelter if she managed to escape unless she could find her way to her closest neighbor. She prayed no Searchers had gone to look for her there.

When at last the dusk lowered, she eased along the side of the house, painstakingly crawling from shadow to shadow cast by the building against the fitful moonlight. The skin on the back of her neck itched, expecting a heavy hand—or a boot—at any moment, but she gained the outer edge of the trees without incident. Shivering and wishing she'd thought to snag a jacket during her impromptu escape, she ignored the growling of her belly and pulled herself up by using a convenient branch. There was a faint glow in the lower window of her home along the east wall, so the Searcher must have located her candles or her precious oil lamp. And was probably eating her paltry supplies.

It was an unnerving trek in the dark, but she knew the area pretty well and did her best to ignore how cold she was, pretending there were no wild animals to be concerned about. After an eternity, she found her way to Johann and Laurel's small plot of land, and sniffed the scent of their stove, following the burning aroma with anticipation. With the scarceness of the local population, finding firewood wasn't a problem, a good thing, considering their frigid winters.

Nothing seemed untoward in the small clearing around their home, so she took the chance and hustled to the back door. A dog barked in warning and it made her start with surprise. She hadn't visited here in a long time, but her neighbors didn't have a dog back then and Lauren hadn't mentioned one. How would they feed the animal? Johann's unmistakable deep voice broke into the baying and then he called out with a challenge.

"It's Celeste." Her teeth were chattering so loudly she could barely form the words, but he heard her. The door cracked open and his tall, skinny body was framed in the archway, a large silhouette of a dog blocking the area by his knee.

"What are you doing here?" Suspicion laced every syllable.

"S ... searchers."

"Are they following?"

She saw the unmistakable outline of a rifle and wondered if he still had ammunition for the ancient weapon. All the newer weapons, both phase, and lasers, had been rendered inoperable, like their means of communication. With the dog and the weapon, Johann clearly expected trouble. "No. They went away, and left one behind, probably awaiting my return."

"Let her in." Laurel spoke behind Johann, and he stepped aside. Celeste didn't wait for him to change his mind and edged past the dog, a collie mix that sniffed her pant leg before slinking out into the yard.

As she entered the small house, the faint smell of their dinner nearly overwhelmed her, and Laurel guided her to a chair, urging her to sit. Her friend was wrapped in a thick robe, fashioned from scraps of material, her hair braided for sleep.

"I'm sorry to disturb you so late."

"Celeste, you're always welcome here, and I'm glad you came to us. I'll fix a plate," the older woman offered, and began to assemble some food from a cupboard near the table. "It won't be hot but—"

"I won't refuse."

"You shared with us all these years, Celeste. Ignore Johann. He's afraid they'll come looking for you here."

"They might," Celeste admitted.

"Not tonight," Laurel scoffed. "Those boys like their creature comforts."

Johann broke in. "They *will* look for you."

"Do you know why? Have they harassed you, Laurel?"

"I think I'm too old, honey. We talked with some of the town folk last week, followed up on those rumors you and I discussed, and there's evidence it's only women between fifteen and forty they come for. But Johann is worried." She cast the man a tender look.

Celeste paused to fork in some cold potatoes and a piece of venison. She didn't normally eat meat, partly because she had no means of obtaining it, but also because she thought animals far better creatures than humans. Yet she couldn't deny how substantial it felt in her stomach. She took her time thinking about the implications of Laurel's revelation.

"Are they ... attacking those women?" She couldn't put a label on what she feared, hoping that particular insanity, and others, were long in the past. To her mind, there simply weren't enough people to go around on the planet to visit atrocities on one another, though she'd seen a few mothers-to-be and no husbands in sight.

"They don't say. No one seems to know. Nothing different than what I told you before. They apparently come back from the government center, and it takes a long time for them to be themselves again, or close to it. Like their minds have been tampered with."

She'd seen the Brownlee girl, the one who shied away and rolled her eyes like a cornered animal, but still didn't want to believe what Laurel was saying. "We don't have that kind of technology anymore."

Johann lowered his brows and pursed his lips. He joined the conversation. "Brainwashing doesn't take technology, Celeste. There are other means."

"I didn't even realize there was an actual government center."

"Someone is taking charge." Laurel shrugged. "There's always somebody wanting to rule. It takes a long time for us to get information here with the dearth of transportation and no way to communicate, but little snippets have been shared in town."

Celeste rarely left her home, unless driven from it, and Laurel had been her main source of information when the woman had come to trade for vegetables. She kept well away from the town, having good reason to avoid its inhabitants. Roy Dupuis lived there, and she wasn't giving him another opportunity to play games with her feelings.

Swallowing the last of the meal, she thanked Laurel and realized her body had warmed up, being so near to the stove. Johann poured her a cup of some dark liquid from a pot simmering on the hot surface, and she sipped at it, indulging in a brief, but fond memory of actual cream in her coffee. Not that what she was drinking was coffee.

"I'll fix you a bed." Laurel bustled toward the hall.

Johann frowned at his wife. "You'll bring trouble down on this house."

"If they didn't know she escaped them, they'll think she'll be back. If they should find her here, they'll believe she was visiting. And where would you have her go?" Laurel made it sound so reasonable, and Celeste wanted to hug her, although felt she should protest.

"I shouldn't."

But Laurel was already finding a quilt and pillow for the piece of furniture that served as their couch, and Celeste stumbled from the chair to the makeshift bed. She couldn't suppress a groan as she sank onto it and Laurel draped the quilt over her.

"We'll see what we can figure out in the morning," Laurel said quietly, and Celeste thought she'd be asleep in seconds, but her mind jittered and fretted.

Johann didn't seem to grasp how she'd survived. And she had, if that was what one could call it, first losing her sister, then her brother, followed by the deaths of her parents. Violence, lack of food, disease, and heartbreak had all taken their toll. And now she was alone, no family, no friends—except for Laurel—and a few folks she might cautiously call neighbors. There were times when survival was highly overrated.

The recent appearance of those small groups of men seemingly tasked with kidnapping women for no apparent explanation had added exponentially to her burden. In truth, Celeste expected the women were taken as sexual fodder, something she was going to avoid if she had to take her own life. Which brought her back to getting out of her current situation, and *surviving* another day. She gave her head a tiny shake, the fleeting memory of all the ancient vids she'd watched as a child with Maury and Alice, huddled in their family home, before the loss of technology … those reminiscences could gut a person. There were no more cowboys to ride to anyone's rescue, no heroes to save the maiden.

She lay there, the lumpy couch a welcome substitute to the littered soil beneath her window, and reflected on the events of the past several years since the invasion. The aliens had arrived when she was young, and it was hard to think about all the intervening years, full of such terrible losses and huge life changes. Now, at the ripe old age of twenty-three, she was alone in this world.

It wasn't anything like the old movies depicted, not the *War of the Galaxy* or even the comedic *Uranus Attack!* There were no giant spaceships as shown in *Earth Decimated* or any other science fiction show. Earth had already been decimated by the Great Plague of 2084 and the terrible nuclear accident in Asia, and hardly worth the time of such a powerful race of aliens. Celeste thought, if it had been up to her, she would have simply passed on by the sad remains of her planet, but perhaps the Meridians had seen something worth salvaging.

The invasion had been quite hands-off, and eerie. First off, all communication had been disabled in some mysterious manner. No computers or cell phones worked, nor landlines, not that there were such a great number of those, there was no radio or television—all technology simply failed.

Shaky interim governments were brought to their knees, and predictably, if one knew humans, and perhaps the Meridians did, everyone turned on one another. And then, if word of mouth was true, the aliens simply went away.

Perhaps it was like playing God, she mused. Survival of the fittest. Subdue a planet and its inhabitants by robbing them of anything but the bare basics, come back in, say, a thousand years, and see what was what. As sleep crept up on her, she wondered what those aliens were up to now.

****

"Master, we have searched most thoroughly, and there is only one species that is truly compatible with our kind. Even if mere coupling with many of the others we've sampled would not be an issue, should one be inclined and willing to overlook some anatomical differences—or celebrate them—none of them are capable of becoming pregnant with Meridian offspring. At least not without considerable gene splicing and certainly not within the time we have left. There is only the one species that suits, and there appears to be a complication. Resistance and outright interference from the inhabitants of the planet have been reported, and considering its nature, it can only be the result of someone from Meridia sharing our intention." Bast shook his head, his lips set in a tight line.

Lysett shoved his hand through his hair and released a weary sigh. Well over a year had passed since Trosan's death, and what he'd hoped to be an uncomplicated task had proven onerous and frustrating. He had given the mission of finding envoys to General Ashtun, following that meeting after his concubine's demise. That male found trustworthy individuals to travel to the planets Bast had located, starting with the closest planets after Bra'oor. DNA and other samples were taken from females. Lysett had no doubt much of the sampling was covert and done without even the females' awareness. He chose not to concern himself with the minutiae or the subterfuge. Desperate times meant desperate measures.

He had been determined to keep Bast's search private and expended considerable effort to keep the matter confidential. Those opposing him, however few, would use failure against him. And even if he succeeded… Well, they'd still take up the cudgels, citing racial purity or some such. But despite the attempt to keep the missions classified, there were still a fair number of individuals aware of parts of the bigger plan, and quite able to draw the inference. Those special envoys and the scientists tasked to examine the evidence were pledged to secrecy, but Lysett knew a secret remained a secret only until told to a second person.

"I had faith in Ashtun's ability to command obedience, but considerable time has passed."

Bast shrugged. "Indeed, enough for some to process our intent and decide if this is something to challenge your politics with, Master. Stirring unrest on primitive planets is an easy thing to undertake."

"It might not be only about politics." He paced the room, recalling his visit with the General—Liasion Ashtun.

The flight to Bra'oor had been uneventful, and he'd wished for some sort of diversion, an issue with the instruments, a surprise meteor shower, even a space pirate attack to deal with. Instead, he was left to his own devices and worse, his own thoughts, and he tortured himself with additional memories about his childhood and growing up with Trosan.

He eschewed the honor guard upon landing and was quickly escorted to meet with General Ashtun. The highly decorated officer was in place as more of a formality, considering the actual passivity of the population, and Lysett nearly regretted coming to Bra'oor. It spoke of a lack of confidence in the General's abilities and he hoped the man had understood the need to cloak his real intent. He'd endured a long, tedious lecture by the General's aide before he could sit down with Ashtun.

"I thank the Ruler for taking the time to honor us with his presence," the General's aide had kept repeating, and Lysett knew it was grating on Ashtun's last nerve as well. The aide was a political appointee, from a smaller but powerful House, and it wouldn't have done to alienate the man.

At the end of the presentation, he accepted an

invitation to a very decent meal, tastes, and textures of Bra'oor he likely never would have enjoyed if it hadn't been for this impromptu trip. It served to remind him of Bast's announcement about other species possibly being compatible with their kind and encouraged him further. This led to an in-depth conversation with the General and some of his officers about other species and even touched on future assimilation.

"For the most part, our settled planets are stable and without any signs of discontent, Ruler. Bra'oor is a good example of our more recent excursions," the General concluded. "Expanding our territory will expose us to other species, and we can afford the manpower given the stability. I salute your rule, Sir."

Lysett had welcomed the broader point of view, albeit from the perspective of the fighting man. It had been years since Lysett had been on the battlefield, although he continued to train and keep himself in shape. Ruling didn't mean losing touch with those who put themselves at risk in both the defense of Meridia and the necessary off-world campaigns. Lysett, at heart, was a warrior, but he needed to consider the future, and one without violence was the better concept.

"I would hope to hammer out trade contracts and build alliances as well as invite travel and commerce between worlds, rather than add to our conquests. Perhaps encourage interplanetary liaisons and consider interspecies ... connections."

The ensuing silence was smothering, and he wondered if he'd misinterpreted the mood of these men who surrounded him.

The General finally spoke, after quickly scanning the room and then clearly choosing his words carefully. "A future concerned with rebuilding the population of Meridia, saving our species, would be an accomplishment of the highest order, Ruler."

The murmurs and chatter that followed had reassured him, once they'd processed such a foreign concept. It had been a test, and one he was glad he'd carried out. Those were the men who would bring about his will and reassure the populace, and Ashtun had found his envoys among them. Several raised their cups in his direction and he found himself lifting his own in return.

The General had pressed his hand in the traditional way for a significantly longer period of time than usual, and Lysett recalled the other man's widowed status. Warriors didn't necessarily show softer emotions, but he sensed the commiseration. It had made him all the more determined to find a solution—find compatible females.

"There will be those who will oppose you, Sir," the General said quietly. "But you may count on me."

"I leave Bra'oor in your capable hands, General, until the final treaties are filed," he had said formally. "I will have need of you in the coming months if we are to implement changes."

His last sight as he boarded his transport was that of Ashtun's calm features, laced with anticipation and perhaps hope. To some extent, it soothed Lysett's beleaguered heart and aided him during the ceremony to celebrate Trosan's life.

He'd told Bast to promote General Ashtun, and put him in charge of recruiting those sent to procure future concubines. To title him Liaison.

His servant had made a note, and there was no further talk about Lysett's impromptu trip, nor about the far more pressing issue of finding a compatible female to serve as his personal royal concubine. His first servant had known not to waste his time until there was something to present, and was well aware of the distinctive interest his Master had taken in the process. The discussion had then turned to politics, Lysett's focused mind having considered certain alliances between minor Houses, and also on future events requiring his attention, and he'd began to rebuild his life.

He yanked his thoughts from the past and gave all his attention to Bast, who again watched and waited patiently, aware of his Master's way of processing especially momentous decisions.

"Tell me," he ordered his first servant.

"Do you recall the planet named Earth?"

Sifting through his mental files, Lysett nodded. "We conquered it over a decade ago, if one could call it conquering. The populace was already decimated and nearly doomed, so the decision was made to thwart their remaining technology and leave them to rebuild slowly. Give the planet a chance to heal, as it were, and consider it an outpost in the event we required a planet to stop by and resupply. Are you saying…?"

Bast stood and stretched, then pressed his screen, projecting an image onto the far wall. "Indeed. That most primitive place and one at the far reaches of our System has compatible females. It was by accident that an envoy took specimens there when he did, because Earth was near last on our list, and likely another ten months or more before any sampling would take place. His ship was thrown light years off course after an encounter with a rogue asteroid and forced to land for repairs. I understand he disembarked to walk about and happened upon a young female."

Lysett studied the primarily blue planet for an instant before turning his attention to the outline of a female figure juxtaposed in the image. He reflected that while somewhat smaller, it appeared to mimic the shape of Meridian females.

"Continue."

"I don't know all the circumstances because I haven't yet spoken to him. Sardan is his name. Of one of the smaller Houses, but holds a solid reputation both as a warrior and now as an envoy. He is a widower as well, and I suspect had puzzled out the true reasons behind the sampling. It seems he took the initiative and possessed the DNA as well as the ovum."

Lysett held his breath. Both procedures sounded intrusive. They *were* intrusive, ethically, although with their medical technology it was doubtful the young female had even known what had taken place. He arched a brow at Bast, willing him to continue.

"The DNA is startlingly close to matching, so close our scientists suspect that whatever seeded Meridia, seeded Earth as well. Both of our species adapted to the differences in the environment, and advanced at different rates, obviously."

"And the ovum?" Meridian ovum was not viable in the laboratory, despite all their vaunted technology, hence the inability to grow test tube babies. That might have been their answer instead of asking female Meridians to accept a veritable death sentence. Or to advance on this quest.

Bast's face fell. "It appears healthy, but when infused with our sperm it is also not sustainable in the laboratory. We only have the sampling of the one female, of course, and it is difficult to extrapolate, but our scientists are most certain Earth females can birth Meridian babies. We simply require more data."

"So sample more." Lysett nearly growled the order, but Bast grew somber.

"That was our plan, Master. We sent out many envoys. However, the planet is very sparsely populated after their wars and plagues, not to mention the chaos that ensued when we dissolved what little technology remained. Females of childbearing age are few in number, and more difficult to find than one might anticipate. Then, there is the complication."

"Explain."

"Word has clearly gotten to Earth about a search for compatible females, Master." Bast shook his head and quashed Lysett's next question before he could voice it. "We don't know who spoke it, though it, of course, had to come from one of the other Houses, but a kind of centralized government has recently formed on each of the populated continents of Earth.

"It appears propaganda has been circulated about our race once again descending upon the planet, and this time impregnating all females. Conquering by populating their world with our offspring—committing genocide in that manner. And it has created some kind of strange reaction."

Lysett pondered the information. As an efficient way to conquer, it made powerful sense. If an invading force visited its offspring on the female population, that action would change the face of that planet. It wasn't the original plan at all, of course. Any compatible females would have been offered the opportunity to leave their primitive Earth and take up residence on Meridia, to live in luxury and be cherished, worshiped as life-bringers. And surely those females who remained on the backward planet were true survivors, fit and healthy to have weathered the adverse conditions.

"What is the resistance you speak of?"

"The information is fragmented, and not totally validated, but we believe all females of childbearing years are being rounded up and either brainwashed to reject alien advances, or are being sterilized."

Hearing the latter was like a punch in the gut, and

Lysett fought for breath. Impossible. What kind of creatures did such a thing? *What kind of creatures in Meridia's past focused on conquering other planets and taking that which appealed to supply—oversupply—their people's physical needs while ignoring the falling birthrate? And look at the way we—I—made the decision to tumble Earth backward to mere subsistence in the event Meridia might use the planet at a later date.* He shoved aside his conscience and organized his thoughts to sum up the situation.

"So we approach a non-sterilized female and she rejects us because of the brainwashing, leaving us no recourse but to kidnap her and try to change her mind. A reprehensible choice, considering how far we've come from the bloody conquerors of our past. Or, worse, we find none who can conceive because of the actions of zealots. Xenophobes like we were—and still are in some regard, obviously, because you're right. I definitely detect Meridian influence here. There is no such thing as a coincidence, Bast. I want an investigation into this sabotage. All resources. Put General Ashtun in charge of this as well. It will tie in with his present work."

"*Liaison* Ashtun."

Despite the circumstances, Lysett nearly smiled. Ashtun had been a good choice for Liaison, a new role in Meridia's history, but the other male chafed at the relative sedateness of his position and longed for action despite his support of Lysett. This exercise in addressing sabotage would no doubt turn bloody, and Ashtun was the right man for the job. They had become friends over the past while, once the Liaison had gotten past the difference in their station. Lysett had needed a strong friend who understood the same issues, and Ashtun fit the bill. Not to mention his ally's hope for his own concubine. "*Liaison* Ashtun," he agreed.

Bast nodded in understanding and paused before continuing. "I suggest we make contact with every female on Earth of childbearing years and determine compatibility without delay. But of necessity, we must alter our original plan."

"Go on."

"It will mean gathering them all without ceremony and interviewing them in a place of safety, like on one of our ships. We can return those to Earth who refuse us for any reason. Unless..."

Lysett considered the implication and decided. "Every effort is to be made to encourage the fertile females to come to Meridia. Every effort, Bast. We'll sort out the ethical issues later but won't waste any more time. We are fighting an invisible enemy at this point, and must take every advantage."

"I thought you might say that, Master. I advised Liaison Ashtun already, and he ordered his troops to land on Earth some time ago. We should have reports in shortly."

Bast had never overstepped before, not in all their years together as Master and first servant. He anticipated but hadn't superseded his Ruler's authority. Lysett bit back his immediate reaction to dress down the other male for his temerity, then accepted how the urgency of their situation transcended the chain of command. This wasn't only about him and his House, although no one wanted civil war—he hoped. This was about countless other males who wanted a concubine for procreation and therefore the perpetuation of their species.

The remaining Meridian females would no doubt feel both relieved and unimportant, but Lysett already had some thoughts on that subject. One thing at a time. All the same, he added another order, spelling it out carefully. His first servant blinked, then accepted it without comment, his clever brain obviously processing and drawing conclusions.

Chapter Two

The Searchers didn't show at Johann and Laurel's place, although Celeste supposed they could have come and gone, or even held a meeting in the very room she had slept in, without her knowing. The stress and tension, her heavy thoughts, as well as the cold, exhausting trek to her neighbors had taken its toll, and she'd been oblivious until Laurel woke her late morning.

"Johann went to check your home, Celeste. There's no one there." Laurel looked hollow-eyed with anxiety.

"He shouldn't have done that. What reason could he have given? What if they had hurt him?"

Her friend couldn't meet her eyes, and set a cup of the erstwhile coffee on the rickety table, paying an inordinate amount of attention to her action.

"Laurel, what happened? What's wrong? Is Johann all right?" All of her questions tumbled out, fraught with fear and worry, but she thought she already knew, and resigned herself to hear the answer.

"He's fine." Laurel absently rubbed the ears of the dog, who'd crept in to lean against the other woman's legs. Finally, she looked Celeste in the face. "There's nothing left of your place, honey. They burned it. It's pretty clear they don't want you to have any place to hide out."

For a long moment, Celeste held still against the news before taking note of her crumbling innards, and the sickening feeling of despair. "God."

"You'll have to stay with us." Laurel moved away briskly, perhaps recognizing that Celeste required a little space and time to put herself back together.

All she had were the clothes on her back and a small trinket of her mother's she always carried in her pocket. The chain of the locket was broken beyond repair, but the filigreed silver heart held her family's painted visages and was always on her person. There wasn't much of worth in her home, but it had provided shelter, and the land, sustenance. It was quite the final blow, insofar as strikes against her went, and she didn't know if she could weather it. But what choice did she have?

"I can't stay here, Laurel. Johann will protest, and he's right to think I'll bring trouble down on you. I'll have to go into the town."

"But that's probably what the Searchers want."

Laurel was likely correct, but maybe Celeste could mingle and fit in, and find out why women were being targeted. Hopefully, there was safety in numbers and they might think she'd already gone in for that processing if she learned more of how to behave. She might be able to circumvent whatever was going on and stay out of it. She could act like the Brownlee girl.

"I'll take my chances."

"But what about Dupuis?"

Well, crap. She didn't want to consider him in the mix. "I won't have anything to do with him."

"He'll see it differently, Celeste. He treats all women under thirty like they're his personal toys."

And gets away with it because he's handsome, well built, still has all his teeth, and washes frequently. Plus he makes a living and can feed himself. Celeste smothered an inappropriate laugh and realized she was over her teenage infatuation with the man. It had been a stroke of luck to see him with that redhead back of the store, the woman on her knees before him while he had oral congress with her. The graphic tableau had shattered her young, inexperienced dreams and hurt her pride, causing her to eschew the town ever since.

"I won't fall for his sweet talk," she said, determination lacing her tone.

Laurel looked at her assessingly. "You're over him."

Celeste belatedly wished she hadn't confided anything about Roy to her neighbor, even the little she had, but Laurel had been the only woman she felt she could talk to, and being lonely was a true hardship. "I think I've been over him for a while. I learned a good lesson anyhow." *Not to fall for the superficial.*

"Well, that's a good thing. Hanging onto a lost love isn't healthy."

Snorting, Celeste said, "Well, it's not like I'm spoiled for choice, Laurel. How many available men are there anyhow?" And she wasn't inclined to fall in love—or even consider it—when she recalled how devastated her mother was when her father died. In fact, her parent had followed soon afterward, having no interest in carrying on. If that was what love did to a person…

"Good men are few and far between," the other woman agreed, "though the strong and clever have survived. It's still hard to believe that the population took such a hit because of the plague and then the wars in reaction to the aliens. I sometimes think it was meant to be. I mean, we'd overpopulated our world and consumed so much of its resources. Not to mention the pollution."

Celeste didn't want to get into a discussion about the olden days, and who knew what the stats were now, in truth? It *was* true that those still alive and functioning were made up of strong, determined stock to get this far, but at a terrible cost. Life still pretty much sucked, and she had a future to plan. Sipping at the coffee drink, she accepted another plate of potatoes and venison from Laurel, sharing a few bites with the hopeful dog, before making her way to the outside toilet.

The bucket beside the shack was rimmed with ice and she shuddered as she washed up, drying off with the clean rag her friend must have hung out for her that morning. Her brain churned, just as it had over breakfast, but came up with nothing other than heading into the town and looking for some kind of work. She could sew, after a fashion, she could cook and clean, numbers came easy to her, and she was a good gardener. She wasn't above doing any kind of honest work. Maybe her prospects weren't so dim.

Laurel was sorting through some clothing when she re-entered the house and held up an old denim jacket. "This should fit. And there's a sweater, as well. I'll find you some gloves, but it's good you have your boots."

Winter was coming, and Celeste was glad she'd stopped to shove her feet into her heavy footwear before scrambling out of the window—was it only the day before? "I appreciate it, Laurel."

"If things don't work out in town, you come back here. Johann will just have to accept it. I can't see you struggling when you've been so good to us."

Johann hadn't been adverse to accepting produce from her when he and Laurel had first moved here, but he wasn't as inclined to give back. He was a morose individual, but one who clearly cared for his wife. If Laurel *was* his wife. The chances were they'd met up in the refugee drive from one of the defunct cities, and connected. It didn't matter. They were a loving couple in a time when there was little enough of that commodity. She quickly steered her thoughts away from her parents again. It scared her silly to think of loving—and being loved—like that and having it torn away. Definitely not for her.

"He's protecting you, Laurel. I get that."

"You're so mature for your age, honey."

"Not much choice. I've been on my own for a long time." *And it would feel incredibly awesome to have somebody ease my burden and look out for me.* Like that would happen, and how perverse was she in her thinking anyhow? Only people who loved another did that.

Shrugging into the jacket, and tying the sweater around her waist, she accepted a small packet of food from Laurel. With an impulsive hug, she whispered her thanks in the other woman's ear, before skirting the dog and heading out the door.

The fallen leaves crunched beneath her feet as she walked the deer path toward the rutted foot trail that signaled the approach to the town. She'd taken a quick detour, finding her way far more quickly in daylight, to see her house with her own eyes. Johann hadn't lied. The place was nothing but an unwieldy pile of charcoal. There was nothing at all left to salvage unless she wanted to sift through the smoldering ruins, and she didn't have the time. The loss made her heart clench, just another in a long string of them.

Her borrowed jacket was open over her shirt as the afternoon sun warmed the soil, and she should have been picking up the pace. Instead, her boots scuffed and dragged in the debris, while she willed herself to be optimistic. Surely there was a place for her in the town. She had to eat, and she required shelter, so despite the abject poverty of the area's inhabitants, so hopefully there would be someone to offer her work. She resolutely didn't think about the Searchers and the rumor and speculation around what might be in store for her, yet her survival instincts desperately pushed her to turn back and run pell-mell to Laurel and Johann's. Except it would cause strife between the couple and in the end, Johann would see her gone. Returning there would only prolong the inevitable and bring trouble down on her friend's head.

Squaring her shoulders, she traversed the last few yards and trod up the grade to the road, squinting ahead to see if she could sight the town of Belford. And stumbled to a dead halt, the dust around her boots eddying out in the sudden silence. Not that it was actually quiet. Her footsteps no longer sounded, but countless others seemed to reverberate in the distance, and there was no mistaking the muffled feminine protests and deeper, more masculine shouts. Her heart began to beat again, pounding in her temples as the blood surged throughout her veins, and she stole one, then two, cautious backward steps, trying to take in enough oxygen to make her lungs work.

In her shock and fear, she forgot about the steepness of the grade, and her left foot scrabbled for purchase, seemingly independent of the rest of her body before it turned under her weight. With a stifled cry, she toppled sideways and rolled down the slight hill, each and every stone and protruding root imprinting on her skin, wherever the fabric of her clothing was vulnerable. Her little packet of food skittered away in her peripheral line of vision, the ends of the tied-off cloth fluttering as if in farewell.

Coming to rest at the bottom, she lay, disheveled, and paralyzed with fright. Holy hell. She hadn't seen a lot of them, and she'd been really young, but the memory of those vids of Meridian ships wasn't something that faded with time. Spaceships were supposed to look like saucers, or maybe like the Earth rockets, and not such a graceful, yet menacing, mode of travel. And the figures surrounding the ship were obviously taller than most men on her planet, despite the distance from her present position and them. Her mind had cataloged the entire scene in that moment before her retreat and wrestled with the fact there were other humans amongst the aliens, struggling as they were escorted, or dragged, toward the spaceship. Female forms, primarily.

Celeste stared up at the autumn sky, such a bright blue, with wispy mare-tails of clouds, an impossibly clear view of normalcy, when one considered what was going on just down the road. Her heart continued to pound within the confines of her chest, although her breathing was more within the normal range, and she carefully moved all her extremities, wincing at the pain in her ankle. She eased to one side, pulling her knees up, then rolled onto all fours. Unwilling to risk standing on what might be a sprain, not to mention anyone—any alien—seeing her head pop up alongside the road, she began to crawl for the shelter of the trees. This was fast becoming an unfortunate turn of events, and she didn't care for it at all.

She didn't hear him coming, not over the crackling of leaves beneath her hands and knees, nor over the pounding in her temples, but surely someone of that size couldn't have moved so quietly. One minute the line of trees beckoned, the next they were blocked by a pair of enormous black boots and heavily armored legs, a type of long weapon pointed down beside the right knee. Scrambling ignominiously sideways, she risked a shove to her feet, the abused ankle protesting mightily as she did so, but her attempt at flight was for naught. A big gloved hand caught her bicep and hauled her against a wide, solid chest, her face smacking into some kind of belt across his shoulder. She cried out as her ankle absorbed the additional pressure and her cheek met the unforgiving armor. The alien stilled.

"My apologies, female. Where are you injured?" It was a deep voice, speaking in halting English, and she could feel it resonating from his chest, his breath feathering across the top of her head.

She couldn't respond, too busy trying to manage the loosening of her bladder. She wished she remembered how to pray.

"You must answer," he insisted, and she detected a note of concern despite her fear, and remembered he'd apologized. This was so the *Twilight Zone*, those strange black and white movies recovered from the archives— back when there was technology.

"My ankle and … my cheek. Mostly." Her response sounded breathless and rife with terror, but she was past pretending.

The alien set her slightly away from him while supporting her weight, and green eyes scrutinized her face. She cast her own gaze down, trying to breathe, and searched for more words.

"I'm fine. I'll just get going." She made herself look him in the eyes. *Never show fear in front of a predator.* Who had told her that? Or had she read it somewhere? Maybe it was one shouldn't stare at them lest they interpret it as a challenge. Heaven help her.

"That is not the plan, female," he said formally, with a deferential nod. How could he appear respectful when she was so obviously at his mercy? "I will carry you to the ship to spare your ankle. It and the slight abrasions on your skin can be treated immediately."

"No, it's okay. Really. I don't live far from here and … and my mom will help me out…"

"I have my orders." She was swung up as if she weighed next to nothing, and cradled with care against that broad chest, then carted back up to the road and toward the ship. He made the climb with minimal effort and the show of strength silenced her.

The activity had dwindled, with only a few of the taller figures in view, and one of them strode to them.

"Report." Another alien, dressed the same as the one toting her along, although with heavier markings along the shoulders, spoke to her captor.

"I heard a cry ring out and the sounds of a fall, Commander. I investigated. This female fits within the parameters of our search. She has injuries."

Celeste heard a distinct snarl emanate from the other alien, and the one holding her tensed, before speaking again. "The leg injury and the other marks happened when she fell, I would assume, and I take responsibility for the one on her face."

"She is a potential life-bringer!"

Holy smokes. A person could cut the tension with a knife, and she didn't like being between caught between these two individuals. They were both strikingly handsome, with features much like those of some of the Earth men she had known, although these two had eyes of virtually the same green color. Siblings? Her mind jumped to the thought of clones, another outlawed advancement tabled in the archives.

"I will accept discipline," her personal transport announced, and she found herself unable to swallow the words that bubbled up. He probably didn't need defending, but she was nothing if not fair.

"I tried to run, and he grabbed me as my ankle gave way. I fell into him. It wasn't his fault."

Alien number two froze in place and transferred his gaze to her. Green. Green for sure. Black hair like the other guy, green eyes like his. With pupils like a cat's. She shivered as they elongated as his stare locked with her own. He then nodded—deferentially. With respect. What *was* this? *Life-bringer*?

"As you say, female." He turned back to alien number one. "Bring her. She is the last in this area, and the transports from other parts of this continent are away to the mother ship."

She didn't want to go. And the fact she was the *last* didn't bode well, especially when there were apparently other transports. It didn't take a genius to recognize what was going on here. Alien Abduction 101. Resistance was futile, however, although once she was on board that ship there was a good possibility she'd never see Earth again. Or perhaps she would return, changed and different, probed and maybe possessed. She tensed in the alien's arms as he marched to the entry of the vessel. This behavior reminded her of the Searchers, and her stomach roiled, its paltry contents souring with every connect-the-dots thought she had.

At the last minute, she struggled against the muscled arms holding her captive, striking out with both fists and trying to flip her body free. She didn't waste her breath screaming for help, or begging, but simply tried to get away. But he merely tightened his grip and the other alien, presumably his superior, spoke over his shoulder.

"You must accept this, female. You will not be harmed. And you will receive an explanation shortly, as well as the best of care."

She didn't want to accept being kidnapped, although sensed they actually meant her no harm or would have not been so careful with her. It was the promise of an explanation that settled her, however, and she subsided. It was that or admitting she had no choice, and was powerless, something highly unpalatable. Denial might save her sanity for the time being. Her alien transporter carried her deep into the bowels of the spaceship and she heard a hiss behind them as the light from her planet dimmed with the closing of the hatch. Her emotions shut down tightly with the sound.

****

"Do you know what's going on?" The question

was posed by a really tall brunette with wide, hazel eyes.

Celeste had been surveying her remarkably healthy ankle. There was no sign of swelling and only a slight discoloration across the arch and around the joint itself. She hadn't yet put her boot back on, in fact electing to take both of her footwear off and walk barefoot to the area she was presently sitting in. The flooring was immaculate and as smooth and warm as anything she'd trod. Not that she really had much of anything to compare it to.

The alien had taken her to what was clearly a medical treatment room, although she hadn't seen anything like it since her youth, and carefully deposited her on an exam table. Her terror had resurfaced, all those ancient stories about vivisection and sampling surging into her forebrain, but another alien, maybe a doctor, had simply waved a device over her. Her cheek was now fine, and all the little cuts and bruises had vanished. She'd explored the surface with her fingertips, looked in the proffered mirror, and saw no evidence she'd scraped the skin. Her hair was another issue, tangled and full of detritus from the ground. She'd been loath to brush off her clothing in the seemingly sterile surroundings, but twigs and leaves had sifted off of their own accord.

The medical-type alien had assessed her quickly, speaking reassuringly, and with respect. Once the injuries were treated, aside from him pressing lightly on her abdomen with a silver tool and then taking a blood sample, she'd been released. There were other women in the same room being attended to by other male aliens wearing the same kind of clothes, but no one seemed to be in any real physical distress.

It wasn't her imagination that the guy who had caught her looked relieved when her wounds were dealt with so swiftly, despite how quickly he'd masked his features. She'd asked his name, offering hers first, and in apparent shock, he'd supplied it. Janler. No last name. Maybe it was his one and only, although he'd said something about a house. A trooper. And he'd quickly brought her here before departing with another of those nods. *Here* was a large room with a door that didn't open from the inside, occupied by a number of other women.

Trying to smile at the brunette, she shrugged. "I don't have a clue what's going on. I just got escorted here. Are you okay?"

"I think so. I arrived a few minutes ago. I saw a doctor type, and he extracted some blood, prodded at me, and then I was brought in to join them." The other woman gestured around at the young women of all shapes and sizes and coloring. They huddled in groups of twos and fours, with the occasional individual perching alone on the seating scattered here and there. Lowering her voice, she asked, "Do you think they're going to perform some kind of experiments on us?"

Celeste had already homed in on the blood sampling, fingering the area near her elbow where the fluid had been taken, because there was no longer an obvious site of retrieval. She looked at the other woman's arms and saw nothing to indicate anything on her skin either. To say the room wasn't vibrating with anxiety would be a lie, but none of the others were carrying on in any fashion to suggest hysteria, and that struck her as strange.

Women had come to accept their lot over the years, in a time where might had made right. They'd either become a partner, like Laurel, if they were lucky, or some man's chattel, or, like herself, had forged a path alone. So maybe this wasn't a place for screaming and freaking out, but surely the reaction around her was unusual. Come to think of it, *she* was pretty calm on the face of it. The terror she'd experienced upon witnessing the kidnapping of other people and then herself had markedly dissipated, and yet she didn't feel resigned to her fate.

"I don't have a clue," she repeated. Staring into the other woman's eyes, she detected curiosity mixed with puzzlement and thought she probably looked much the same. "I think they gave us something to keep us from acting up."

Brow wrinkling, the brunette slowly nodded. "That makes sense. Although there's another area out there sounds like a bunch of cats are locked inside."

Some of Celeste's calm bled away. "What?"

Nodding again, the brunette blinked owlishly. "One of the armored guys was leaving it as I passed, and the noise was horrible before the door slid shut. There were women in there."

Shivers returned, and she clasped her arms around herself in an awkward parody of a hug. The other woman mimicked her and actually rocked a little, forward and back. Celeste's imagination ran rampant and she visualized what was going on in that room and wondered when her turn would come. Experiments. Rape. Did the Meridians *eat* people? Clone them? She felt the urge to rock as well.

"I'm Shirley Janson."

"Celeste Raynor."

"I can't handle this." Shirley's words were edged with burgeoning hysteria and it spurred Celeste to a decision. She was tired of things taken from her control.

"Then let's do something." At Shirley's startled look, she shoved her feet into her boots, then stood and clambered on top of the bench-like seating, balancing with one hand against the smooth wall of the craft. "Hey!"

It required two more loud calls before the rest of the women paid attention. And then they focused on her like she was intensely important. It made her innards quail because she usually avoided attention at all costs, but the information from Shirley about that other room had tripped something inside of her.

"I'm Celeste Raynor and I'm not going along with this … this atrocity."

A murmur began with another tall woman in the corner, who stood and drew up the other two women she'd been crowded together with. Other voices joined hers in agreement and most of the others got up and moved to gather closer to Celeste.

Taking a deep breath, she asked, "Does anyone know why they grabbed us?"

There was a chorus of denial and some shaken heads.

"Were any others taken that you know of? Who aren't in here?"

A blonde spoke up. "I saw a couple of others from our village, Charlotte, and Moira. They aren't here." She hesitated before adding, "They lost it when escorted away. And I mean lost it. It took a couple of those big guys to subdue them. Do you think they're … dead?"

"The woman from next door went the same way," a high-pitched voice contributed.

"I saw a few others like that," another woman called out.

"Me, too."

Celeste couldn't sort out all of those who were offering the information, but she heard Shirley say something again about the other room with the upsetting clamor. Thinking fast, she wondered if there was some way to make a stand, some previously unknown warrior part in her raising its head.

"Hey!" She punctuated her shout with a shrill whistle. This time, everyone paid immediate attention. "Shirley here says there's another area, a place down the hall, that doesn't sound so good, what with the noises coming out of it. Maybe that's where those women are."

The tall woman pushed forward, her red hair glowing in the overhead lights. "So they grouped us according to behavior?"

"Maybe."

"And what are they doing to the ones who got crazy on them?"

Celeste had no answer and didn't want to venture one.

"Charlotte and Moira were kinda frail. Their dad took them away a couple of weeks ago, and when they came back they never left the house. He said they were sick. Maybe that's why they went nuts." The blonde shook her head. "I heard rumors about an alien invasion from a guy who was in the old city. He said there was a movement afoot so none of our women would be good captives."

A couple of the women began to cry and were quickly joined by several others. Celeste figured the invasion had to be related to the Searchers abducting women, but couldn't think it through. Things were deteriorating rapidly and she figured if they didn't have something to occupy themselves, all of them would soon be in that other room. She cursed her initiative and wondered how to fix it.

Whistling again, she succeeded in gaining their attention. "I'm thinking they gave us something when they took that blood sample. Something to keep us placid, the ones who didn't go crazy on them first. Maybe it didn't work on the others. But I'm not going down without a fight."

"We don't stand a chance," replied the woman who had expressed concern about her friend from next door.

"Maybe not, but I'm not going to sit around like some docile animal while the Meridians decide to do what they want with us. If they drugged us as it is, to keep us calm, I'm not going to let them do anything else without standing up for myself."

Her little speech played back in her head, and Celeste experienced no small shock at her temerity. Regardless, it seemed to appeal to the rest of the women and they looked to her, apparently waiting for direction.

"I hardly think they'll come in here one-on-one, to take us someplace or…" She didn't know what else they might do, so stuttered to a halt, not willing to speculate. There were enough horrible thoughts in her head and not all of them about aliens. "Anyhow, if we break into groups of say, five, with somebody in each group who has been doing some kind of manual labor, to kind of spearhead with strength, we should be able to take on up to three of those troopers."

There was some strangled laughter, and one woman said, "Most of us work hard, honey. Just like it's obvious you do. Groups of five should work. We just blitz them and take 'em down."

"And if they use their weapons?" That was Shirley, and Celeste couldn't blame her for her reaction, seeing as she'd been so unsettled by what she'd heard from the other room.

Another voice interjected. "What if they do? We're probably dead anyhow, and in ways I don't want to imagine."

"I don't think they'll use shooting weapons on a ship," Celeste said, remembering the old space series she watched all those years ago. "And they were pretty courteous, overall. I just want off of this thing before it leaves Earth!"

"So we overpower the guards or whoever they send in, and try to get to the exit? I'm Belinda, by the way."

Nodding at her, Celeste scanned the others, who were looking determined and focused, now they'd shaken off the torpor. It wasn't a great plan, because even if they got to the door or hatch, it was unlikely anyone would know how to open it. But it was all they had. They grouped themselves accordingly around the room, with no one appearing to need much direction, and her spirits rose at the sight of them, her sisters-in-arms.

As it turned out, they didn't have long to wait. The worst of it was that there was a distinct hum of machinery and something invisible held them all steady, against the movement of the vessel. With a sinking heart, Celeste understood they were airborne and probably making for that mother ship. Well, maybe they could take hostages and force the pilot to turn back. Or keep them from taking any of the women out of this room and to that other one. Or something.

The door hissed open shortly after the invisible pressure loosened its grip, and three Meridians passed through, each pushing a laden cart ahead of them. The aroma of some kind of food permeated the air before the closest three groups of women descended upon the aliens, bearing them down beneath their weight. All without a rehearsal. Celeste wanted to scream with laughter at the heaving figures on the floor as the males struggled to get out from under the scrum. Her reaction was so inappropriate she knew for sure she'd been drugged.

She hustled past the closest melee and managed

to brace her back against the door panel before it slid shut. Shirley shoved a cart her way and the panel stuttered impotently against the barrier as she wedged it lengthwise. The corridor outside yawned emptily and Celeste made a decision while her pulse raced and she quivered with anticipation. Levering over the cart, she crouched and peered both ways, the battle behind her raging on with grunts and feminine squeals, as the aliens were pinned to the floor. Belinda joined her, clambering over the imposed barrier, then Shirley, and a handful of others. Some of the women hung back and peered through the opening.

Hesitating, not willing to leave anyone behind, she wondered how to manage it when movement caught her eye. Several troopers, sans weapons, and wearing far less armor, were moving swiftly in their direction. As if on cue, Celeste chose the point, with Shirley and Belinda at each shoulder, two others at her back, and they charged the first trooper. It was the alien who had chastised Janler, and she allowed herself a moment of satisfaction as the wedge of women bore him to the floor. She heard whoops and screams behind her as the rest of her sisters piled through the door.

Chapter Three

"Master?"

"What is it, Bast?" Lysett was on his way to see his parents and was running late. He never seemed to have enough time anymore, primarily because he chose not to allow himself any.

"Part one of the mission is complete. All the compatible females we located are off the planet Earth and en route to the mother ship for the interviews."

"Good. Let me know—"

"Master?"

Ah, so there was an addendum. Of course, there was. Nothing ever ran smoothly.

As if reading his mind, Bast added, "The process went as planned with the exception of one of the transport ships. I thought I should raise it."

The underlying excitement in his first servant's voice gave Lysett pause. He gestured for the man to continue.

"No one was badly injured, although there were some bruises and contusions, and certainly some damaged pride. But the prize…" Bast visibly swelled with pride, his chest out and shoulders back. "Ruler, this is a warrior race of women when given the opportunity. Think of the offspring from such a joining!"

"What?" Lysett thought his roar of a question might have been heard in the far reaches of his dwelling and sought to calm himself. "Explain. And assure me none of the females were among those injured."

"No, Sire. Forgive me. I should have been specific." Bast blinked his eyes and gave Lysett an anxious look. "We gathered nearly one hundred women—ninety-eight—from several small towns and surrounding area on the large continent where the weather fluctuates wildly each season. Regrettably, twelve of the women lost their minds upon being taken and had to be sequestered and medicated. The remainder were more docile and were given a mere hint of an anti-anxiety drug to ease the transport."

As much as he wanted to know more about the warrior race of women, and vastly relieved none had been harmed, Lysett inquired about those twelve who had gone insane.

"They will likely be returned, Master. The brainwashing appears irreversible in the short term, although we believe once back with their kin and away from our troops, they should settle down." Bast was somber as he relayed the information. "And of those remaining, only fifty-nine were fertile. Eighteen of those were sterilized, and had apparently been willing to undergo the procedure."

"So the propaganda was effective," Lysett reflected bitterly. "Twelve life-bringers too terrified of us to even hear what we offer, consider joining our ranks, and eighteen frightened into taking precautions to avoid bearing our children. Irreversible damage, even for our technology."

"Yes, Master. And the numbers are no better on the other ships, but there are still several thousand prospective females on their way to the presentation and the offer we will make. But we know at least forty-one of them have proven warrior status, so there is no doubt there will be more. The sedation was increased for the remainder on the other ships to avoid altercations and circumvent risk to the females."

Many Meridian females had been formidable warriors in the distant past until they became too valuable to risk in battle, by virtue of their gender and dwindling numbers. And the children of those females had risen to lead the most powerful Houses in the past. Lysett inhaled a deep breath, his hopes increasing as he released it. "Have you ascertained females who fit the criteria of my House?"

"I have, Ruler. Tentatively. The most likely female is the leader who led the women in their siege on our troopers. She is fertile *and* pure. The other tests have yet to be performed. And there are several others who meet your specifications thus far."

He turned his attention back to the *minor* troubles on the one ship, and allowed himself to pursue it now, rather than consider having a female to breed. Trosan's striking face rose up behind his eyelids and he forced them open, again breathing deeply to manage the sorrow.

"What happened in the siege?"

Bast outlined how the women, who had responded to the mild sedation, and didn't display the abject terror of the dozen necessarily confined in the specially designed medical bay, had plotted to attempt some kind of escape. Lysett swallowed a smile at the description of those troopers conscripted into delivering food, being pinned down and held by several females working in tandem. They'd been handicapped by the need not to injure any of the females in any way, and forced to act subdued until someone relaxed their guard. Even then it was difficult to gain their feet and herd their would-be captors safely into corners of the chamber and keep them under watch.

The ones who used the distraction to escape had been swiftly met by other troopers, led by the ship's commanding officer. One of the females Bast selected to offer for his Master was responsible for taking that male down. Certainly not alone, and with considerable effort, but while no females were harmed in the resulting furor, many of the troops sported bloody noses and blackened eyes, not to mention sore genitals. They were apparently the favorite target for the warrior women, and Lysett hoped his troops had all been wearing armor to mitigate those blows.

"I believe they were trying to take hostages and bargain to have the ship turned around. But they were restrained and their interviews will be conducted by our teams on the mother ship." Bast smiled with pleasure.

Despite the entertaining story, and everything going to plan, Lysett couldn't muster up much anticipation. The thought of another female—even a warrior—didn't appeal, and while he would do his duty, it would mean betraying Trosan's memory.

"And what of the plot to derail our plan?"

Shaking his head, Bast replied. "Liaison Ashtun has yet to report any progress on that front. But he won't abandon the task. He has set troops in secret among the populace, a difficult strategy considering how few the humans are in numbers, and the necessity to adjust our spies' appearance.

"His intent is to protect further brainwashing attempts. And I know he is searching closer to home. He also believes the plot started here."

"Then we'll leave him to it. But ensure there is a choice of concubines for the Liasion."

"Certainly, Master."

He wondered if Ashtun would also struggle with the idea of taking another concubine, even if it was in the best interest of Meridia. The other man, too, had lost his mate, and her with child, as Lysett had come to learn.

"Lady Trosan would approve of this, Master. She of all Meridians would see populating our planet again as a wonderful opportunity." Bast's kind words still grated, but Lysett heard the abject pain behind them. Again he wondered if Bast had felt something for Trosan—

Shoving up from his seat, Lysett ordered, "If the female who led the others meets the remaining specifications and accepts the offer, then she is to be well prepared, both mentally and physically." A virgin concubine was a prize beyond all others and he wouldn't see the woman maltreated, especially if she lived up to his standards. "And ensure she understands the contract with the royal additions. Do not speak of it again until everything is in place. If she refuses, begin consultations with the others."

Bast's voice was void of any inflection as he answered. "Of course, Ruler."

****

Of all the things Celeste had imagined, the offer set out by the Meridian presenter guy, Cleros, was the last thing she expected. After the aborted—and poorly planned—attempt to force the ship to turn back and let them disembark, the women had been returned to the same room. They were encouraged to wait against the hull while the carnage of the upturned food carts was cleaned up and taken away, and further refreshments delivered, but no harm had come to them. There weren't even any threats made against their person in retaliation.

While the troopers guarding them viewed them with wariness, there was no visible desire for retribution on any of their faces. If anything, Celeste saw respect and admiration written there, accompanied by the occasional rueful grimace when the males moved. She'd landed a solid punch to the groin of the alien she took down, and his nose was still swollen. Apparently these fighting men eschewed medical care for such trifling injuries. Like men all over, she reflected, remembering how her brother Maury ignored superficial cuts and bruises. The one he couldn't ignore had become infected, and he'd died moaning and out of his mind with the poison … but she wasn't thinking about that now. She was reflecting on the offer. The one she and nineteen others from her group had accepted upon being transferred to this mother ship.

"So, you accepted, too." Shirley's voice was quiet and disembodied in the darkened space of the sleeping room. "I hope it was the lecture that appealed and not something they gave us to influence our agreement."

Celeste wondered about that, as well. The offer seemed too good to be true, but with the conditions back on Earth… Yet surely some of the women had family there.

In a nutshell, the Meridians were looking for breeding stock. Oh, it wasn't couched in those terms. Rather, it was an awesome opportunity if the presenter was telling the truth. Nothing was said about why the aliens wanted to expand their bloodlines, but she suspected it had to be for very good reason, in order for them to lower themselves to purloin a few fertile gals from primitive planet Earth. She hadn't missed the faint hint of scorn and contempt for her world and wondered if the others had noticed it. Not that she should have any loyalty to a place that had killed off the majority of its population and picked off her family, one-by-one.

It was the other information that had really convinced her—and the rest of her sisters-in-arms. It had to be true because it explained the behavior of the Brownlee girl and the other two women the blonde—Jessica—had expressed concerns about. The Searchers were on the hunt because of the Meridians' desire to make babies with Earth women. Someone in charge had decided that humans weren't going to participate—probably a male someone, because the actions taken were out of fear, disgust, and ignorance, the usual human reaction to outside influence. It didn't excuse what had been done to countless women.

There had apparently been several thousand brought aboard the huge vessel, all of child-bearing years. A quarter had been brainwashed to the extent that they went catatonic upon even being approached by a Meridian trooper, and some had willingly agreed to earlier sterilization to avoid bearing an alien offspring. All of those women had apparently been returned to Earth, something she fervently hoped was true, and not put down like rabid animals or something. A fleeting thought that perhaps it might have been kinder, considering the state of her world and the people populating it, was dismissed instantly. She couldn't let herself go there.

"Celeste?"

"Sorry. Just thinking everything that led up to this. I don't believe we were drugged by that time or hypnotized. The offer seemed sincere."

"I thought so, too, but it's a mess either way. And it would have been better to be approached back home, where we could have discussed it with others and made the choice."

While Celeste didn't support the outright kidnapping of those of her gender, she positively hated the reaction of Earth's de facto governments. Typical paternalistic assholes. How had they thought to populate Earth, for heaven's sake, that they offered—likely encouraged—sterilization? And would brainwashed women ever want to have sex, having been scared so badly it might mean being forced by any male? What would happen to the children of such unions? Heads so far up their keisters…

"It wouldn't have been safe. Not where I was from. I'd be one of those crazy women now if they'd caught me." She couldn't repress a shiver. "I think this is the better deal, considering the way women are being treated back home."

Bedding rustled as Shirley moved around in her bunk. "It's a chicken and egg thing, though. If these aliens had passed Earth by, maybe things would have been different."

Their situation had been brought about indirectly by the Meridians, but Celeste had nothing to return home to, and the fact the town she'd been headed for was now virtually bereft of fertile women meant the men would be a very real threat to those left behind. And to those being returned. She'd voiced that concern to the alien presenting the options to the throng of women who gathered to hear him out, and he had listened. In fact, he had made a note and assured her steps would be taken to address her apprehension. She hoped to believe him. "Can't change the past, Shirley."

"Well, you seem to be dealing with it pretty well. I guess I'll take a page out of your book and work on my optimism." The other woman made a huffing sound, part laugh, part sigh, and left Celeste to her thoughts.

It wasn't lost on her that many of her original group viewed her as a leader of sorts, and while she was content to fall back into the ranks, it wasn't always possible. Other women sought her opinion and her counsel, and she processed the information herself in open discussions with the others. The language barrier had been overcome with tiny earbuds, with the interpretive devices to be surgically inserted later. Women from all over the world now mingled, something Celeste knew she'd never have seen on Earth. Groups formed and separated, most splitting along age and cultural lines, but there was some overlap. If Celeste had to count the women now on board, women in all shapes and sizes, she'd estimate a few thousand.

Concubines were highly respected, apparently revered on Meridia, and in no way viewed as sex slaves. This had been strongly emphasized and repeated. A few of the women had relaxed enough to crack jokes about sexual slavery not being a hardship if all the aliens were as good-looking and built as the troopers. Frank sexual conversations took place, accompanied by anatomically correct drawings, and there were no surprises on that front unless one considered that the aliens were really big—all over. Celeste covertly surveyed the other women and wondered what kind of experience they had with sex, seeing as she had exactly none. One couldn't count Roy's grabbing at her breasts and one sloppy kiss. How she'd ever seen anything in the man...

It was pretty darn scary to be hurtling across the galaxy on the route to an alien world, and there were times she'd thought to ask for some of that sedation the Meridians had utilized upon their capture. There had been an apology for that as well, and a most sincere one regarding the physical examination in the medical room.

A wave of that wand-like thing, that press on her belly, and a blood sample hardly seemed intrusive, but in truth, it did irk the majority of the women, including Celeste, when it was revealed the procedure had determined who was fertile, and who still possessed a hymen.

She understood the sedation from the aliens' perspective, especially given the chaos created by the reaction of those brainwashed, but the other was high-handed. And it meant crushing any hope of those who hadn't been sterilized, yet now knew they couldn't conceive. Although they got to go home—but to what? And what was the comment about virgins? Likely the Meridians wanted to go where no man had gone before, and she wasn't sure how she felt about that. It was all very tiring to think through, and she questioned if honesty was always the best policy.

If she remembered ancient Earth history correctly, any female marrying into the royal families of old had to submit to an examination to ascertain fertility, and reading that had made her sneer, despite how the world had changed, and not for the better. Far worse, she now admitted to romantic hopes, having changed her view about love, considering everything she'd recently experienced. She kept thinking about the love her parents shared, no matter the state of their lives. Even Laurel had something with Johann. Celeste knew it was perverse, and probably a reaction to thinking herself lost, then presented with a better future. But it was unlikely she'd find love on another planet when the matches were all about a contract, and she now decided she wanted something she couldn't have.

Ah, she couldn't dwell on the past. With so little to recommend Earth to her, she'd agreed to take the offer and become a concubine. It felt surreal, but then nothing about the past few days was the least bit normal. It wasn't as if she'd been going to find someone on Earth anyhow.

She accepted her new position and would soon arrive on an alien world and find out what was expected of her. Like she didn't know. Broodmare. Well, she liked kids and never expected to have any, considering her situation, so that might be okay. And if the Meridians held up their end of the bargain, then at least she'd be taken care of, and there were worse things in life. Even if she had no real choice.

After all the hollow reassurances, finally shoving the feeling of being powerless into a small part of her brain, for now, she curled up in her designated sleep bunk and tugged the covers up over her ears. The large room she'd been assigned to held perhaps a hundred women, and the sounds of the others either slumbering or thinking their own thoughts surrounded her, and sleep overtook her battered senses. She eventually fell into oblivion, much the same way as the time she'd fled the Searchers.

Morning came, and she groggily rose with the others and used the facilities, shuffling along in the queue. It became apparent this was a huge operation, and someone knew a thing or two about organizing. Once showered, they were provided soft pieces of clothing, a loose top that pulled over one's head, and a skirt that wrapped around the lower body to fasten at the waist. There was a length of fabric that alternately parted and joined with the help of some kind of sticky material. She learned it was to provide support to her breasts, and there were underpants fashioned out of thinner material that seemed to stretch to fit everyone. Everything was in a pale blue, and she thought the apparel made all the women—the concubines—appear remarkably similar, despite their difference in coloring, shapes and sizes. It was vaguely disquieting, and she hoped it didn't mean they weren't allowed to be their individual selves.

"You still okay with all of this?" Belinda asked the question, but Shirley was right beside her, looking the same query with her eyes.

"Mostly."

"There's nothing for me on Earth," Belinda confided. "I heard you talking with Shirley last night. My dad went off to find work and never came back, and I wasn't able to earn enough to keep everything going. I figured I was going to have to whore myself out anyhow. It's not like I don't know what it's about."

"It's not whoring," Shirley cut in. "It's not. My

mother would die if she thought I was a prostitute."

"It's whoring." Belinda put it out there.

"Maybe on Earth," Celeste said. "But unless they're lying to us, we're going to be sort of like wives there. Maybe even better than wives, at least compared to how it was back home for lots of women. And monogamy will be the rule. Besides, we have the right to refuse the guy who chooses us if it doesn't feel right. And if we aren't treated well, we can appeal, and be matched with someone else." *Except we can't go home.*

"That's what he *said*." Belinda's voice inferred disbelief and not a little scorn. With her thick red mane and curvaceous figure, the other woman commanded attention.

Celeste bridled her tone because it was too scary not to consider they'd been fed a big pile of horse poop. "You don't believe him?"

"I don't believe much of anything. But like I said, there's nothing back there for me, and it was only a matter of time before things went to complete shit. So I signed up. Maybe I'll get an offer from a stand-up guy, but I'll figure it out."

Shirley winced. "Well, I think it's an opportunity. I wanted a family and it'll be nice to have enough to eat and be able to see a doctor and stuff. Maybe even somebody to take care of me. The guy I was with wasn't the best."

That's what Celeste secretly hoped for, too, but she didn't say it. Instead, she supported Shirley in her desire for children and agreed about the advantages portrayed on Meridia. Belinda smirked but didn't press the matter, her cat-like green eyes glinting with cynicism.

The remainder of the day passed with more information being shared about their new home, punctuated by meal times. The women were gathered in groups of a hundred or so and ate and studied in different rooms that appeared to have been prepared to accommodate them. The mother ship was huge, and Celeste appreciated the presence of a guide as they moved from different points.

A crash course on customs was provided over the next several days, and everyone was given a small, square item with a screen that responded to touch. Celeste was fascinated, recognizing it as an item similar to old technology on Earth. Not that it could in any way compare. So much was at their fingertips and she immersed herself, glad she enjoyed reading. Meridia had an amazing history, as bloody and violent as Earth, but was now far more advanced and cultured. It hadn't fallen prey to the diseases and uncontrolled warfare that had ravaged her home world, and while the politics seemed confusing and unpredictable, it appeared that as a conquering race, the Meridians now ruled a huge section of the galaxy without discord.

Celeste understood the concept of propaganda. Earth had apparently used it most recently to interfere with the aliens' plans to propagate with humans. So she was aware what she had read could also be written to skew the reader's viewpoint, and she doubted all the information had been supplied. Humans, and probably aliens, tended to hold things back if it suited their cause. She supposed only time would tell, depending on how much she was allowed to participate in life on the planet. So many unanswered questions.

There were lots of conversations with the other to-be-concubines. Some Celeste didn't care to dwell on, seeing as most were far more aware of what they were getting into insofar as the physical side went. Others expressed the same thoughts and questions as she held, and for the first time, she enjoyed being with others of the same sex and age group. Laughing and talking hadn't been a part of her life and she was glad to have the opportunity. She stomped hard on any whimsical hopes about the alien who might offer for her, but it was difficult not to be a little optimistic when life was rolling out like a grand adventure, if a rather frightening one. The lick of anticipation was somewhat arousing.

"Your attention." Cleros raised his voice over the cacophony of feminine ones and slowly the tide of chatter diminished. "We will be entering Meridia's atmosphere in one Earth hour. If you have any final questions, please approach."

Soft slippers rustled against the deck of the ship and glances conveying too many different feelings to catalog were exchanged. A few of the women stepped forward, but the majority kept their place, including Celeste. She wasn't plagued by anything other than who would choose her, and that question wouldn't be answered until at least tomorrow after they were settled in. And even then there was some kind of preparation period with the guy, maybe like a courtship humans had indulged in before her time.

Shirley eased alongside. "I feel sick to my stomach."

So did Celeste, but she preferred to think about it as butterflies. "It will be fine. We can always refuse." *And what if the next male is worse? What if this is a really bad idea?* She wondered who was looking at her file and her picture even now, and deciding to offer for her. At least no one should be left on the shelf, considering the apparent need for females there.

"It's not a bad feeling, really."

Startled, Celeste studied Shirley's face, but the other woman was peering at the warrior who'd been in charge of the kidnapping—resettlement sounded better—

of the women from her town. The one who'd been so outraged over her injuries. Commander Adares. Celeste realized her friend perked up whenever the warrior entered the room and recalled his covert glances in Shirley's direction. She pressed a hand to her own belly and wondered if she'd be drawn to a Meridian she might hope to accept…

Chapter Four

Meridia was nothing like Earth. Not even close. The sky was mauve, for one thing, and there were two suns, in a red-gold shade. From Celeste's viewpoint, the smaller sun appeared to chase the other across the sky, spraying hues of darker purple in its wake. In contrast, the soil was golden and the water—Meridia had a lot of water in the form of lakes, rivers, oceans, and streams—stretched out in placid vats of violet. Coupled with the bright-lime vegetation, it was almost too much to bombard the senses, except the housing was pale gray with slightly darker roofs and the streets and walking paths a soothing taupe. She sucked in a deep breath and tasted freshness and cleanliness with a faint bite of salt.

"Isn't this something." Shirley was looking about with an expression of awe likely mirrored on Celeste's face.

"It's quiet. And clean. Manicured yet with a hint of wildness."

"Aren't you the poet," her friend teased. "Better than your place on Earth?"

"Everything there was so overgrown and unkempt. It smelled clean and fresh, though, what without transport to foul the air. Sort of like here, I guess."

"The town I lived in wasn't so clean. And pretty sparse. These dwellings look … rich."

"Well, we were told the inhabitants here don't lack for anything." *Except for children.* Maybe that was why it was so quiet here, though not like the solitude back home. That was something she chose.

The Commander, following Cleros's order, had formed them into groups of a hundred or so and sent them, with heavily armed escorts, into varied sections of the city where she understood the majority of Meridia's inhabitants lived. Most of the male population were stationed throughout the galaxy, revolving home for periods of time. There weren't huge numbers left, in any event, and the majority of them were male. That was the truth, if the few females she'd seen since arriving were any indication, unless they kept them sequestered. But so far, Celeste hadn't found anyone to be lying to her.

Their technology was very superior, at least to that of Earth's and presumably other species in the System, because despite their dwindling numbers, the Meridians ruled far and wide. She could understand they didn't want their race to die out, not like humans who had essentially destroyed the planet and one another. She thought she could understand why the Meridians nixed Earth's technology to force them to stand down, except it backfired. When given the opportunity to rebuild, her people had squandered it, in Celeste's mind. Someone else had asked an important question on the ship some days past, the one niggling in the back of her mind.

"How did people on Earth find out you Meridians were coming for us?" the thin blonde named Tracey asked Cleros.

Celeste felt the tension as the rest of the women became quiet and the silence stretched out. It was the first time she sensed anything that wasn't assured and confident.

"We aren't certain, but it's something we are investigating."

Another woman spoke up. Celeste had stood on tiptoe but couldn't see who it was. "So somebody didn't want us coming your way."

Cleros sighed and nodded. "We have xenophobia here on Meridia as well, young female, and there are

*politics on any world. The current Ruler wishes
concubines from your planet to procreate with our males
and thus we carry out his orders, but not everyone
agrees."*

She remembered the anxious swell of sound filling the room as she and the rest of the women muttered. She appreciated the honesty because it meant they could be on their guard. If certain Meridians were opposed to those orders, the women could get caught in the middle. The warriors in the room inched forward, but their demeanor illustrated no ill intent, but rather, concern and protectiveness. Nothing untoward had happened on board to her knowledge, but she fervently hoped there were no xenophobes among the Meridians nearby. Or someone with a different political agenda than the current ruling House. Or a combination of the two.

"Hey."

Celeste blinked when Shirley waved a hand in front of her face. "Sorry. Thinking about the idea not everybody wants us here, and the way our fellow humans addressed that problem."

Her friend inclined her head. "No sign of us not being welcome, though. At least not among those who greeted us. Before the Commander dispersed us."

Shirley's tone was bitter and Celeste tried vainly to read her. "What's wrong?"

With a shrug, the other woman replied. "Not so different than Earth, honey. We might be real important here, but that doesn't mean we get to choose."

"We can refuse." Celeste hung onto that point.

Huffing, Shirley paced away, then turned and stared. "That's not what I mean. I didn't return to Earth, I signed the contract, and agreed to the interview. But the one I want ... he walked away without a word and I'll probably end up with somebody I hate."

Celeste didn't know what to say to that. She had no idea if the Commander was eligible for a concubine. Cleros had spoken about measures to determine who would be allowed to choose, and maybe the warrior wasn't one of them. What if that happened to other women … and her? What if they fell for someone and couldn't be with them? Shirley was obviously miserable.

"Did you tell him how you felt?"

"Of course not. I mean, look at him. And look at the choice he has now. From nobody, to pretty much any of us. Risking rejection isn't high on my list of things to do. It rates right up there with being kidnapped."

"Maybe you can talk to the person in charge."

"And say what? I'll take the Commander, please? We might have the right to refuse, but there was nothing about choosing. It's them choosing us."

Celeste couldn't help think about Roy and the redhead. There weren't enough human females to go around here, at least she didn't think there were, but what if these guys were like Roy? She shook her head and shoved the thoughts away. Cleros had assured all the women that there would be a match for all of them, eventually. He didn't talk about cheating but inferred fidelity and the outlined contract supported it. Maybe the dearth of females promoted monogamy with these guys hanging onto the woman they were lucky to land. The idea of being shared didn't sit well with her at all. Somehow she doubted any of the women would be allowed to refuse to join with some male on this planet, but time would tell.

"I guess you're right, but I'm hoping for the best."

"There's that optimism again, Celeste." Shirley turned on her heel and headed from the garden toward the building that housed the group they were included in.

Someone had named it the Dormitory, after housing provided back when there were schools. Their time outside was over.

After taking another look at the surroundings, Celeste followed, and the circle of guards were but a few steps behind her. There was more studying ahead, and soon the matches would begin.

****

"I don't understand." Celeste studied the Meridian who stood in front of her. His stance was awkward, as though he was uncomfortable, yet his clothing and embellishments indicated his rank and wealth. She had no idea why he would find meeting her awkward.

"I represent the House of Daboort, whose head is the current Ruler of Meridia, and has been for decades, Lady Celeste."

She hadn't been a lady—or at least treated as one—ever. It felt respectful and she liked it. Anything to quiet the butterflies doing free-flight in her belly. But the Ruler of the planet was offering for *her*? How was that even possible? "Okay. And you're saying he is choosing *me*?"

"Actually, the interview you participated in denotes a good match, and the subsequent tests denote your complete suitability. My Master has accepted, er, chosen you as his concubine if you complete the training successfully."

"More training." Studying filled the time and eased her nerves so she'd applied herself, but more?

"Preparation might be the better word," he said, caution lacing every syllable. "Because he is the Ruler."

"So it's different than the other matches?" Many of the other women from her group had been chosen and were presently getting to know the male. Only one had refused immediately. Shirley. Celeste couldn't think about her friend now.

"Somewhat." His tone belied his statement, but she wasn't surprised. It was presumably a great honor in any society to be chosen by the boss.

"You want to prepare me for becoming the concubine of your Ruler before I meet him. Like how to comport myself? Things of that nature?"

She didn't miss the relief that crossed his aesthetic features. This Bast looked more like a clerk or something, hardly a warrior, but he seemed kind. He was also anxious and she supposed being sent on a mission for a monarch with a chance of failing might weigh on a person. Hadn't the kings of old Earth cut off peoples' heads?

"Yes. That's exactly it, the reasons for the extra training. Will you accompany me?"

"Where are we going?"

"To the Ruler's abode. You'll have an apartment there during your education."

She still couldn't believe the Ruler of Meridia had chosen *her* and she wanted to ask Bast why, but the part of the contract outlining the primary reason for such a match danced through her head and she dispensed with fripperies. The interview had garnered her personal information and there'd been a variety of questions that turned her head inside out, but this wasn't about how she looked or the way she acted, or who she was. It was about being fertile, and being a virgin probably didn't hurt her chances any. A Ruler might have those standards. A pure broodmare. It made her unaccountably sad to think he had no need to meet her first.

"I need to say goodbye to someone." It wasn't like she had anything to pack, except maybe her boots. She raised a hand to trace the chain around her neck.

Janler had fixed the twisted and broken links, and the locket fit safely behind the soft fabric of her top.

"As you wish." Bast smiled widely and indicated he would await her.

Shirley hugged her hard and wished her the best, but it wasn't difficult to see the misery behind the good wishes. "Let me know how you're doing, Celeste. See where all that optimism got you? I hope he's gorgeous. Head of the class, girl. I knew you had it in you."

"I'm not sure I was supposed to tell you who chose me, Shirley." Maybe she should have checked with Bast.

"I won't tell anyone until you agree, Celeste. No point in causing any problems. Not that you'll refuse, probably."

"I'll keep in touch. And get a message to me when you are matched." She didn't want to talk about her apparent good fortune, not when her friend wasn't happy.

She waved a final farewell and hurried to meet Bast who flickered a glance toward her boots but courteously offered to carry them. "I'll take those, my lady, and perhaps you'll tell me why you look so … sad?"

She was hardly going to tell him that being a broodmare might represent a comfortable life, far better than the one she left behind, but that it also felt cold and distant. As though she was a commodity. Besides, Shirley was *really* sad. "My friend? She cares for one of the warriors who kidnapped, I mean, picked us up on Earth, and hasn't seen him since we landed."

Bast frowned, and she immediately changed her opinion. This man might not look like a warrior but he could be downright scary, and he radiated power. "He took liberties?"

"No. Not at all. But they were … looking at one

another while on the ship. And Shirley developed some feelings for him. She's been offered a match but refused, and I expect it's because she'd rather be with the Commander."

"Commander Adares?" Her companion's voice was sharp, almost commanding.

"I'd better not say anything further."

"Not at all, my lady. I personally feel there could be … more to the matches if we didn't rush into things. What is your friend's name?"

Halting, she waited for him to stop and face her, searching his features. "What will you do with it?"

"I promise you, nothing untoward."

"Shirley Hyde."

Bast fished a square screen from a pocket of his tunic and tapped on it. "I have her." He showed Celeste a picture and she nodded.

"That's her."

He tapped a while longer and made a quiet, satisfied sound. With a smile, he tucked the device away and offered his arm. "We don't have far to travel. I thought you might want to walk, but I can arrange a conveyance."

"Absolutely not. I like to be outdoors and active. Will you tell me what you just did? About Shirley?"

"I merely arranged for the Commander to have an audience with someone who can make special dispensation for those who do not have the immediate right to offer for a concubine."

Celeste knew he'd chosen his words carefully and decided not to press him further. She'd be checking with Shirley and find out straight from the horse's mouth.

They walked in relative silence for a few minutes with Bast pointing out things of interest and importance, such as the marketplace and the governing building on the horizon. "The Ruler spends a great deal of his time there."

Celeste noted the presence of several large warriors flanking them but keeping their distance, and made out even more stalking along in front at intervals. She wondered if Bast needed bodyguards or if they were for both of them, but didn't want to ask after only just meeting him. It would be something she would inquire about in the not so distant future because it had occurred to her this Ruler would make a prime target for those who disapproved of having humans as concubines. It had been his decision, after all.

"You like children?" The question yanked her from her thoughts.

"Excuse me?"

"Not to be indelicate, but you are here to procreate, Lady Celeste. I merely wished to confirm the fact you indicated in the interviews that you liked children."

Sadness washed over her again but she squinted up at the suns and pretended the reddish light was making her eyes water. "I like children, as I told Cleros. I never thought to have any, though, until this happened."

"So you didn't leave someone behind then, not someone you cared about."

She stopped and faced him. "If you're aware of my feelings about children, then you know the rest. I was eking out an existence with little hope for the future. So you Meridians coming by wasn't the worse thing. Although I fear even more for Earth's recovery, now."

Bast met her stare, then nodded gravely. She wondered if this was some kind of a test of her honesty when he inexplicably picked up the pace. She matched her steps to his, picking up on his anxiety. Her belly tightened. They continued on a few hundred more yards before turning into the courtyard of a huge dwelling with stark and simple lines. Separated from its neighbors, it had great appeal if it was a little intimidating, and she let Bast sweep her past the plantings and up the broad steps. They were ushered through two large double doors, their forward warrior escorts peeling off in opposite directions. When the heavy panels shut behind them, Celeste stood blinking in the cool dimness. It would have been nice to spend a few more minutes outside, taking in the place that might be her future home, but she felt safer inside.

Bast nodded to a warrior who placed himself in front of the entrance, and she noted how rigid he was, how alert. She turned to Bast, a query on her lips, but he spoke first.

"Your apartments are on the second level. This way."

"Are there any females here?" She tried again to keep up but was a step behind.

He spoke over his shoulder. "No. Our excellent cook resides elsewhere and the meals delivered. We have several warriors, some male servants, and myself who live here."

"And the Ruler?"

"He is usually occupied with governing, as I mentioned, and is rarely home. His residence is in the other half of this abode when he leaves his office. And he also works here, at times." Bast turned right at the top of the stairs and threw open a door a few paces along. "Your quarters."

It was a lovely place to stay. Celeste felt comfortable as soon as she walked into it. Numerous, narrow windows were set into the far wall, allowing diffused light through the gauzy fabric that draped them. One side of the space was set up as a sitting area, complete with a desk and comfortable chairs. The other end boasted a high bed, covered with thick, white linens. Cool tiles flowed beneath her feet, although there were small carpets scattered about.

"It's lovely. I see it faces away from the street." She crossed the room to peer out on a large yard with considerable vegetation. A fountain burbled below.

"It will be quieter."

The streets *were* quiet, something all the women remarked on and she'd noted earlier. So there was another reason Bast wasn't sharing. Impulsively, she asked, "Is it safe?"

He drew back, as though she'd threatened to strike him, before lifting a shoulder. "You are intelligent as well as beautiful, my lady. I expect you have heard and understand the concern that there are those who don't approve of off-world joinings. It is something my master has anticipated and prepared for because your safety and that of your fellow human females is of the highest importance."

"Thank you for being honest with me."

A pained look twisted his features. "I will do my best to be forthright, Lady Celeste, as much as I am able, being the Ruler's confidant. You'll understand the need for some secrecy given my status."

Likely he meant there were things that the Ruler didn't want anyone to know. Least of all a concubine. She could understand his reticence. Her reason for being here was hardly that of a confidante, unlike the relationship her parents shared. "It's fine."

"Please explore and get comfortable. I have a few things to attend to and then I'll return with a meal. We can begin your training."

****

"Your impressions?" Lysett knew he should be

meeting with this female and creating his own impressions. He should be making her acquaintance, aside from knowing only her name, and allowing her the opportunity to know him. But it betrayed Trosan. This was a … business arrangement. His duty.

Bast gave a short bow. "She is bright and learns quickly, Master. She appears to like our world and misses very little of her surroundings. In addition, Lady Celeste has already displayed empathy and likes children. I believe we—you—chose well."

Lysett firmed his jaw and resolved not to inquire about the female's physical appearance. That didn't matter. Everything Bast shared thus far was important. "It's better for a child to be reared by the mother so that's a very good point. How do you know she is empathetic?"

Hearing of Celeste Raynor's concern for her friend and for one of his warriors chipped away slightly at the shield he'd erected against her. "Did you assess the concern?"

"I did, Ruler. The Commander, Commander Adares, had no expectations, a retiring fellow in many ways despite his warrior status. He'd noticed this young woman and didn't find it easy to think she would be matched with another, yet accepted it. As expected."

"We don't want others to see these females given as a reward, Bast, but in this case…"

"Not a reward, Master. Perhaps a recognition of two individuals being drawn to the other."

He scoffed, refusing to give voice to the issue always in the back of his mind. "Love at first sight, Bast?"

"It once was, Master, as we know it from our historical archives."

The quiet response nearly gutted him. Lysett paced to an end table and poured himself a refreshment, drinking the contents of the glass down rather than face his first servant. When he had himself under control he inquired, "So, they are a match?"

"It would appear that they are, one of the first that rings quite true. Others have been placed in the Houses to meet with the males who've offered, and a few appear to have been matched. It remains to be seen if those were made in haste or if there is a significant attraction beyond the physical. We Meridians aren't known to allow our emotions to replace the voice of reason—or lust. Perhaps human females are different, and it is important that they have the right of refusal."

The talk of love at first sight and that of emotional lack made Lysett uncomfortable and he had no intention of discussing them. Especially when he was about to enter into a duty match. He overlooked the reference to the right of refusal because his new concubine would have no call to refuse. Bast would have chosen the best match, and he'd convince her to sign the Ruler's contract, and all would be well. "You say Lady Celeste is also bright as well as being warrior-like? That bodes well for offspring."

"Indeed." Bast's tone was so dry, Lysett stared in suspicion at his servant, only to be met with a neutral gaze.

They discussed Bast's impressions of his future concubine in greater detail and he thought he could like the female, and would respect her for granting him children. Duty and the elixir would carry him through during their couplings should his flesh fail him.

"I will begin her final training about your House and the royal expectations tomorrow."

"How long? I'm concerned about the xenophobes. The quicker she can be presented and calm any concerns the better."

"I would think about another week will cover everything Lady Celeste needs to learn. At least from me. But speaking of xenophobes, we were followed today."

Lysett forgot his softer thoughts and ignored the implication from Bast that he might be required to teach the female certain things as well. "The ones following you were those against the human females being here?"

"Unless they were merely curious, Ruler. But I took no chances. We had a full armed escort and I got her inside when one of them signaled closer contact. She is aware there is danger and—"

"It was a good move to educate the females then, and make the risk common knowledge. Celeste dealt with it?" He hoped she wasn't traumatized, although her actions aboard the ship against his warriors would suggest she wasn't easily frightened. Or at best, not immobilized by fear.

"The females are aware so they can better remain safe. A few are most anxious and some were vocal about the situation, but Lady Celeste is accepting. I fear her lot on Earth wasn't kind, and she doesn't expect much more here."

Lysett liked the sound of this female more and more. He wasn't pleased that she didn't think she was deserving of safety and care, however. "She'll be well protected and you'll provide her with anything she requires."

Bast nodded, his mouth trembling as if to smile, but he remained somber. "Of course, Master. I like her already."

"Prepare her for the traditional joining." Any smile he thought he'd witnessed vanished from his servant's visage. "Alert me when she is ready."

"The breeding pallet? Before you come to know her?"

Exasperated, Lysett threw his hands up. "I don't care to know her personally, Bast. The information you've shared tells me she is brave, resourceful, intelligent, and caring. A warrior among a vanquished species. She is also fertile and willing to give me heirs. Prepare her as previously discussed, so I might complete the contract."

"She's pure. Untouched."

"Another quality for the mother of my children. You have done well, Bast. Ensure she is provided with the elixir to avoid any unnecessary discomfort at our joining."

Lysett was proud of covering all contingencies and ignored his servant's censuring stare. Bast's next comment annoyed him further.

"I will require more time then, Master. If you won't meet with her yourself, I must talk with her about you, as she is understandably curious."

"Then do so." He knew his servant wouldn't share anything with the concubine that wasn't appropriate, and refused to consider the female's probable interest in him.

He strode from the room, considering his plan of action against those who would threaten the human females and thus impede the repopulation of Meridia. Justice would be swift and deadly. He stopped to order another guard for Celeste's door and directed yet another to the garden beneath her windows. Guarding against a real, if nebulous, threat was time-consuming and distracting, but nothing was more important than the safety of his concubine. He didn't give another personal thought to the female in the rooms on the other side of his house, as far away from him as he'd been able to orchestrate. It was enough she met his specifications and would do her duty.

Liasion Ashtun's familiar features filled the vid screen. "Greetings, Ruler."

"And to you, my friend." Ashtun didn't report directly to him about the insurgents. He apprised Bast, who apprised his Master. But Lysett would personally convey his decision about addressing the danger. "When you locate those who plot against our plan, eradicate them."

"Agreed. They deserve nothing less. And it will be done quietly and efficiently."

If he could avoid public reaction to dispensing that justice, Lysett would be grateful. He didn't need any martyrs to plague him during his rule. "Excellent. And Ashtun? Have you found a prospective concubine?"

The Liasion's dark features lightened visibly. "I believe I have if the Goddess is gracious. A female with the most amazing red hair and green eyes, nearly like our own. I confess I was plagued with guilt at the thought of usurping another's chances merely because of my rank, but that fell by the wayside when I first saw Belinda."

"Buhlinda?"

"A different name, but one that fits my tongue."

Lysett found himself mentally repeating his concubine's name. *Celeste.* It too felt comfortable in his mouth. "I'm pleased for you."

"Thank you, Sir. Time will tell, of course. But she hasn't refused me. There have been some refusals by the females of those with a higher ranking, and the lottery system has given the warriors hope, though I suspect there will be many who will surrender their commissions if they aren't refused."

Another technicality Lysett hadn't planned for, though he suspected Ashtun had done so. He nodded to the other man, satisfied that he had such an astute ally. "Deal with those opposed and willing to harm our latest addition to Meridian society, Liasion, and perhaps we can look forward to a full and happy life."

"Your wishes, Ruler."

"Once all the females have been placed, or at least as many as probable, you and this Belinda must attend me and my concubine, Lady Celeste."

"Ah, the small warrior maiden. Her exploits precede her. Belinda was proud to follow her." Ashtun grinned broadly. "Does she please you?"

"Bast has convinced me of her utter suitability," he evaded, noting the way the other man's smile faded, his brows lowering. "I long to see our species perpetuated."

"As do we all." Ashtun hesitated, then added, "Something about Belinda promises to gladden my heart. Perhaps I will feel healed."

Not liking the turn of the conversation, Lysett forced himself to display approval and acceptance. "That is good news. Good luck and good hunting, Liasion."

He closed the connection before anything further was exchanged and scrubbed a hand across his face. He was happy for his friend, but that didn't translate into anything similar for him. Duty. That was his watchword.

Chapter Five

It had been nearly two weeks and she was bored. Bored with her own company, bored with the continual "training", and annoyed that she had yet to even lay eyes on the Ruler. For someone who wanted a concubine in order to assist in repopulating his kingdom or whatever it was, he sure was missing in action. Other matches had a head start on him and were going to show him up. Celeste nearly laughed at how transparent her feelings were, even to herself. She was actually anticipating her debut as head broodmare. Maybe Bast and his training wasn't so boring after all. Except, she could admit, if only to herself, it was the pictures of the incredibly handsome and virile Lysett and the tales of his exploits that piqued her interest. If he was even real!

She hadn't been allowed outside, except for the garden area but once, and she hadn't been granted any contact with Shirley or Belinda, or any of the others, either. She accepted the need to stay close to home. Bast had told her about a few attempts to approach human females and she doubted it was about merely *approaching* them. That sounded too civilized. But he assured her none had been harmed, and increasing numbers had been potentially matched.

While she was glad everyone was safe, she knew they had at least met the males who chose them to be their concubines. The highlight was the news that Shirley had been chosen by the Commander, something she knew Bast had orchestrated. She suspected warriors wouldn't be given first choice, at least not until all the males in the political Houses received their opportunity. Politics were likely the same the universe over. Belinda had apparently been offered for, by someone high ranking, and she hoped the other woman's cynicism didn't mar the match.

It would be wonderful when the Ruler got the danger sorted, as Bast insisted was happening, and she could leave the house, though. Not that it wasn't beautiful, and everyone treated her very well, but she needed to be outside and exploring. Celeste felt her palms itch at the thought of working in the soil and nurturing plants and was glad she could soon indulge in the garden. The farming was done by automated means, although some Meridians tended their own gardens and flowers, and Bast agreed that even a Ruler's concubine could do so—once her studies were complete.

There was still so much to learn. Like the fact the planet teemed with wildlife, yet flesh wasn't consumed here. Some of the other women had groaned at that news and weren't reassured that the food provided would be sufficient enough to make up for the lack. She smiled when she thought of how that reassurance hadn't been misplaced. No wonder these people looked so healthy and were so long lived. Their planet was well, their sustenance contained no chemicals and was both nourishing and healthful. Some of it tasted close enough to meat that even the biggest complainers were silenced. Not that she'd had any opportunity to socialize. At this rate, she'd be attending baby celebrations before she *met* her match. Did they have baby showers here like long ago on Earth?

"My lady?" Bast interrupted her musings. "We have further discussion today."

With a sigh, she took her seat across from him and answered his questions. Yes, she understood the various Houses of Meridia held varying political beliefs but followed the House that ruled. Yes, she had educated herself on the workings and stance of the present House, and obligingly trotted out her knowledge for him.

The House she would be marrying into—well, not exactly marrying, but becoming a part of—was the House of Daboort, headed up by Lysett. She recited the number of followers and the names of the key members of the upper caste including his parents—who she hoped would like her if she ever got to meet them—but her thoughts kept returning to the Ruler. Her future... What *did* she call the father of her prospective child?

"What do I call him?"

"Who? The Ruler?" Bast blinked his green eyes with those vertical pupils and raised his eyebrows at her. "Sire. Ruler. Master. Any of those will do."

"Not Lysett?"

Her teacher's face clouded for a moment before he forced a smile. He avoided her gaze and Celeste's belly fluttered, and not in a good way. While the information she'd been expected to learn and retain had been lengthy and detailed, she'd always been a quick study and thus far had easily satisfied Bast. He was strict, yet kind in his dealings with her, and she thought a friendship was developing. Celeste had accepted the male's explanation that she required additional tutoring and time because of who she'd been chosen for, and today had been the only time she'd questioned it. Maybe she wasn't good enough—

"My lady. Please forgive me. This is a delicate matter and new to all of us. I want you well prepared for this joining and confess I hadn't thought past the educative part."

To the "down and dirty" part, Celeste surmised and felt her cheeks heat. She would have to call this Lysett either Sir or Ruler, if she called him anything at all, until, if, she was invited to be more familiar. She took pity on Bast, shoving aside a silly sense of hurt and rejection. She hadn't even met the Ruler yet, after all, and she had to accept the social mores here. "From the readings and graphics you provided and we what had on the ship, we are not different anatomically when it comes to … uh, procreating, Bast. And I won't embarrass you by being too familiar with him."

Again, he avoided looking her way. Finally, he spoke, "You are a cherished, essential part of Meridia now, Lady Celeste. This is not to say there won't be some difficulties—"

She cut him off, sensing she really didn't want to hear what he had to share. No sense in adding to her trepidation. "There always are bumps in the road, Bast. Of any relationship. My parents married for love and there were still difficulties."

"Ah, then you understand. That this isn't … typical, and my Master isn't typical either, but he is a good ruler and dedicated to his people."

So dedicated he yanked a number of Earth's last fertile—and willing—females to save his people from extinction. It was a sobering thought and one she'd shied away from considering so succinctly. "You've had nothing but good things to say about him."

Bast laughed, but it sounded hollow to her ears. "I likely sound as a merchant selling something in the market. But know how important you are, my lady. I can't emphasize that enough."

He was protesting too much, and if anything, it sparked additional dread. "So when do I meet the Ruler?" It was time to move things along, what with all the information she'd stuffed in her head.

"I will arrange the joining for tomorrow. The healer—medico—has advised you will be at your most fertile for the next few days."

Celeste couldn't swallow, her tongue sticking to

the roof of her mouth. Now the time had come, she wished she hadn't believed she was bored. *Be careful what you wish for...* She willed her vocal chords into action. "Like *immediate* joining? I don't meet him first, get to know him personally—and him, me—first? Spend a little time together, before we..."

Bast shook his head. "This is the way of it, my lady, under the contract and by royal decree. Unless you refuse?"

Wow. The air felt thin and difficult to take in although her lungs labored. She should have asked for a visit with at least one woman who'd taken the final step and become a concubine. She should have gone off her nut and been returned home. She should have asked more questions. She should refuse. But she found she couldn't... Blame it on curiosity or maybe plain old stubbornness. Or the fact she should have known better to expect anything special. To refuse now and return to the dorm, start all over again, well, she'd never been a quitter.

Staring at Bast, who had now fixed his gaze on her, brow creased with worry, she twitched her mouth into a semblance of a smile. It was like jumping into the pond behind her house in the spring, when she craved an all over bath, despite the frigid water. Best to get it over with. "Tell me what to expect."

****

This isn't happening. This is not happening. If she kept repeating those words then surely it would be true and she'd miraculously wake up from this erotic nightmare and in her own bed. Except it wasn't a nightmare and she most certainly wasn't in her assigned bed—or even on her own planet. Although her imagination was fertile—and she'd seen pictures of him—it was unlikely to manifest the enormously good looks and incredible physique of the alien male who was stripping right before her very eyes. Yes, stripping. Removing all of his clothes, not five feet from where she lay on a bed constructed of some otherworldly material that both cushioned and restrained her. Had it only been yesterday when Bast told her today would be the day? No wonder she hadn't slept well, thinking about this. And why did this Ruler look even better in person?

Once he'd overcome his reticence to speak so frankly with her, Bast had prepared her with stories of his Master's need, of his sexual prowess and all the pleasures he would bestow, not to mention that cup of elixir she'd swallowed down.

Being assured it was the planet's best aphrodisiac had her quaffing the liquid as though it were a life saver. Its effects were marked almost immediately as she cataloged an increase in her body temperature and a definite aching in her private parts with embarrassingly obvious lubrication accompanying the throbbing. Even her breasts had ached, the nipples tightening and beading in reaction to the potion.

But the effect had worn off because Lysett had been detained for a considerable period. The delay had given her too much time to reflect on her decision and the strange glowing feelings throughout her body had diminished—until he walked through the door. His good looks stole her breath, and when he began to take his clothes off, she wanted to do shocking, sexual things with him. The emotional and physical swings made her stomach lurch.

Her uninfluenced sexual-self recognized the potency of such a male, and to say she wasn't naturally aroused would be untrue. Her body acknowledged a male suited to her, awash with chemistry and basic animal instinct. It was simply the circumstances that brought her here, and the stark implications of the contract that spoiled their first interaction. Why hadn't he deviated from so-called royal tradition and spent some time with her beforehand? Surely Bast had relayed that even an initial chat would be optimum.

Celeste's heart rate doubled, then tripled, when Lysett's erection sprang forth as his lower garments were yanked down, and dark spots swam in her vision. That part of him was a duskier gold than the rest of his burnished skin, and freaking *huge*.

"Shhh, Lady." Bast's caramel tones spoke soothingly in her right ear, and one of his hands tentatively patted her shoulder. She'd very nearly forgotten he was still in the room with her—with her and his Master, although he had handled the process clinically and indicated he would leave before… "You are prepared for this union, as we discussed. It will be over before you know it, and if you get with offspring this first time, there will be no need for further joinings. Unless you wish them. And to beget other children."

Well, didn't that make her feel *special*? No pressure either. Merely a vessel out here in space, far away from home, to be used. She blinked away the tears that welled in reaction. Where was her voice? She could still say no…

The Ruler paused in his approach to the bed and glared at Bast after he spoke, though that look encompassed her as well. Celeste had never felt so naked—or so vulnerable. She knew what was supposed to happen. She thought she was ready. Not. And to think she'd scoffed at the wait, chuckled about others procreating before this man. No one would dare. Shocking need warred with apprehension.

"You assured me she was prepared, Bast." Lysett's perfect features set in angry lines and those remarkable green eyes now appeared as cold and frozen as that small pond at her home place in the winter months. She tried to use the memory of Earth to distract her, and it caused a homesick shudder to take over her entire body, the gentle clasp of the bed's fabric undulating to keep her in place.

Lysett's attention snapped fully to her in an instant, his orbs now glowing with green fire as the vertical slash of his pupils elongated. His gaze raked her body, lingering on her breasts and the apex of her thighs. Despite her limited experience with men, let alone alien men, Celeste recognized lust and desire and her body responded. Or maybe it was apprehension.

"She is prepared, Master. I do assure you. It is merely that a period of time has passed since we expected you to attend her, and it is no surprise that your concubine is experiencing a trifle of anxiety."

Even with the translator chip, Bast's wording felt off to her, and she decided to add her own voice. *This* was going to happen, this *attending* to her, no matter how she second-guessed her decision, and she believed Bast when he promised she'd be safe here. Having sex—joining—with his Master until she conceived was something she could do. Women did it all the time, had done it over the eons. It wasn't like she was being forced or anything. And she wasn't a prostitute, although that profession got a bad rap as far as she was concerned when one considered women had to survive somehow.

She was, according to the contract, a revered commodity, a virgin concubine—who wasn't going to be a virgin much longer—a concubine who would bear a child for the alien ruler, right? And if the baby was female, she too would be cherished and Lysett would try again to beget a son. And again… All of Bast's teachings slipped through her brain with lightning speed. Celeste shivered and quit thinking about all those possibilities and focused on what she'd been promised.

She would want for nothing, be well taken care of, and ultimately, kept safe. The presenter's words and those of Bast rattled around in her head. Given her past circumstances, it was a no-brainer, and she couldn't go home. Her body was up for it, and her mind had accepted it was the best out of all her choices. So it must be her heart throwing up the roadblock, looking for romance, all because of his pictures and the wonderful things his first servant had said about him.

That was nonsense. Just look at the agony love caused a person. Her stupid heart must be masochistic. This was the best deal she'd get and it was time she said something. There was no way she could go through this process again. Humiliation drowned her common sense. She moistened her lips and addressed Lysett, who was busily engaged in a staring contest with Bast.

"I *am* prepared, sir. Sir. Ruler. I won't give you any trouble."

His eyes froze through to their depths again and his dark brows drew together. She noted his erection didn't flag at all, though. He might be annoyed, but it didn't affect his arousal. The wide head glistened in the well-lit chamber, with his natural lubricant beading at the tiny slit. She had timidly asked if her deflowering couldn't take place in the dark, but Bast refused, saying that tradition didn't allow it. Spread eagle as she was, there was little left to the imagination, and she flushed again with embarrassment and no small shame. Lysett was superbly made, muscled and lean, with broad shoulders, long thick legs, and narrow hips. She was … well, she was short, and small and round, now that she'd had enough to eat. So not like the remaining Meridian females on this planet. And certainly not the cream of the crop of the human females either.

"You were not given leave to speak."

Celeste didn't much care for the way he snarled at her, Ruler or not.

She was confined to this weird bed, on display and at his mercy, as per the royal mating ritual on Meridia, according to Bast. Here at Lysett's sufferance, but valuable, and so surely should be afforded a modicum of respect, even by him! Concubines garnered respect here. There had been nothing in the contract to indicate she remain mute. A small huff of anger and exasperation passed her lips, preparatory to giving him a set down, and Lysett loomed above her.

"You are *not* of this planet, Celeste Raynor. You are *not* to forget that, or your place. You are here for one thing and one thing only. Do we have this understanding?" Those handsome features were taut with fury and his teeth ground together, making a gritty sound she felt all the way down to her toes.

Holy crap. All that reassurance about her worth was nothing more than drivel. He despised her! He might be willing to join with her in order to bequeath an heir, but he hated her, or at least the idea of her. What else hadn't Bast told her? What had she missed? She thought because Lysett needed her, he would treat her with courtesy, maybe even affection. Something shriveled in the middle of her chest, curling in on itself, and this time, she was unable to contain the sudden tears welling up from deep inside of her. Stupid heart. Stupid hope. She closed her eyes and retreated, managing a tiny nod. *Get it over with.*

"Master." Bast's reproachful voice danced on the edge of her consciousness as she found a place to hide, deep within herself.

"Enough. We will try this again tomorrow. Ensure she is prepared, or face the consequences. I require an heir in one year's time, or at the very least, evidence a child is developing in her body."

"I understand."

When she dared to crack her eyelids again, Lysett was gone. Bast pressed down here and there on the bed, and it released her. He drew a robe over her for modesty as she scrambled free, mortified she'd been naked in front of him now the elixir had worn off. He scurried about, gathering up the Ruler's discarded clothing and avoided making eye contact.

"Your master is an ass." At the man's gasp, Celeste wanted to call her comment back. Maybe they really did cut off people's heads here for calling the Ruler names.

She decided she didn't care. Bast had maybe fed her a load of hog slop for reasons she didn't comprehend—and she didn't much care about learning those either. She found refuge in anger.

"Lady Celeste—"

"I hope the Ruler has a couple of back up concubines, because if he treats all women the way he treated me…" She tied the robe with jerky motions, tugging at the fabric in an attempt to bleed off her anger. The jerk probably *had* back up. She wasn't feeling rejected or humiliated. Absolutely not. What she was experiencing was rage, and that man could just go and find somebody else to beget his heirs on. Jackass. Tears burned at the back of her eyes but damned if she'd let them fall.

Bast blanched, clutching the bundle of clothes to his chest. Okay, maybe she was feeling a little humiliated. He'd been in the room while his master had dismissed her like moldy cheese *and* he'd seen her naked. She was done with Meridia's customs.

"If you only give me a moment. My Master has … that is, he has certain responsibilities and—"

"I didn't sign up for this. I could have stayed back home and let Roy Dupuis treat me like crap."

"I don't know who this Roy Doo-pwee is, that you speak of, Lady Celeste, but rest assured the Ruler will not tolerate… I mean to say…"

Where was the sanguine mentor from the past weeks? Her teacher and almost friend? Lysett had clearly upset Bast as well. Unless Bast had held things back from her. Celeste shut her eyes, playing back the conversation while she'd lay spread out like a sacrifice. Of course, he had. Definite hog slop. The Ruler had issues all right, and no amount of preparation would suffice. She shoved the ridiculous hero worship she'd been cultivating to the back of her mind. All of the Ruler's accomplishments, especially his fair and . equitable means of governing, had been touted, including his treatment of those less-fortunate species, and she'd built an exemplary male in her mind. No one was that perfect. She had to swallow the realization she'd made a really bad decision in accepting Meridia's offer—and to compound it, *this* particular offer—and now she was stuck here.

"I'm not hanging around, Bast. I'll head back to my room at the Dormitory as soon as you can take me. Or find me an escort." She'd join the other women who'd refused and had returned to wait for another offer. Surely there were other males who weren't so nasty.

"Might we continue this discussion in the morning?" Bast looked ill, his pallor marked.

She felt sorry for him, despite that he'd withheld, even misled her. Probably his *Master* was going to take his anger out on the man when he broke the news. "We can, Bast, but only to find a way to tell the Ruler you had nothing to do with my decision."

"Perhaps a rest will ease your upset, Lady Celeste."

Uh, no. But she smiled faintly and hurried for the door, intent on gaining her own quarters. The whisper of her bare feet against the cool floor was the only sound in the grand house, but she cast a glance in the direction of the Ruler's apartments, knowing she was running yet unable to help herself.

The personal guard assigned to her, Morat, lurked in the shadows, and she studiously avoided looking his way, certain he knew of the debacle that had unfolded down the hall. Her mortification was likely visible.

Quietly closing the door, she stared around her rooms. There was little to pack, so she decided to leave it until morning. The Ruler could keep all the nice things he'd provided. Ah, who was she kidding? Bast had provided them, and thinking otherwise would simply add to the false impression she had of Mister Arrogant Ruler.

She fastened her locket around her neck, her fingers tracing the links of the chain. Janler was a nice man. Maybe they could get to know one another. After all, Shirley had set her sights on the Commander and didn't want to settle for anyone else. Celeste should look around too. When Bast had approached her, she'd gotten carried away and looked above her station. Her, the Ruler's concubine? Romanticism, and stupid at that.

If she had to stay on Meridia, the odds were she'd be pressured over and over again to accept an offer, so then Janler was at least a familiar face. They could get to know one another, and maybe they'd click. She stepped to the window and studied the garden below. *Jerk.*

****

Lysett felt like a piece of dergoss shit, the scat

of a filthy beast that preyed upon carrion. Better he had struck the little female. He deliberately hadn't looked at her pictures nor any of the vids Bast provided. He'd insisted Bast explain it was the way of royalty to join in that manner when in truth many Rulers before him enjoyed their chosen's company prior to the actual act. Keeping his distance to honor Trosan's memory was the right thing to do, regardless of how badly he felt in that moment.

It was enough to know this Celeste Raynor was biologically compatible, pure, and suitable to bear his sons if the Goddess was kind. His first servant's description of her personality had lulled him into believing he was to bed a formidable female, a warrior possessed of intelligence and a sense of humor, one with honor. No, it wasn't Bast's fault he'd anticipated a tall, lean individual, spare and strong, with plain features that had deterred male interest. Hence, her virgin status because the males on her planet were unintelligent and used their eyes instead of their brains. The fact she had willingly signed the contract in exchange for what he and his planet offered, and hadn't demurred at not being able to meet him first, was evidence enough for him to do his duty. And he'd liked the idea of her.

Seeing her on the breeding pallet, peering up at him with eyes the color of his world's largest ocean, above a small bump of a nose and a wide, luscious mouth... A mane of drifting, pale hair across the pillows. All curves and dips and hollows, her round, lush breasts tipped with such pointed, rosy nipples, her tiny, sweet sex furred with golden hair... The life blood had rushed to his cock with such abruptness it left his brain adrift.

He'd ordered the pallet, seeking to incorporate some of the old customs and bring formality to that which had become necessary. And mating lust had nearly swallowed his good sense and made a mockery of his earlier thought to take down a glass of elixir to ensure his performance. Then his concubine had displayed her fear—nay, her terror—of him and what was to transpire. And his guilt did the rest, causing him to react the way he had. Not that it was an excuse.

After losing Trosan, celibacy had been his preferred state, with the exception of self-pleasuring when his bodily needs simply overcame his bruised heart. Gone were the times of having sex for the pleasure, not that he'd had any liaisons after he'd taken Trosan as his concubine. He had owed her his monogamy for what she'd sacrificed. And that little scrap of—what would they call Celeste Raynor? A scrap of humanity? A scrap of Earther? The sight of her, so opposite of his mental picture, had evoked things in him he thought never to feel, unfamiliar yet inescapably arousing. The ensuing guilt was crushing. If it weren't for the hard fact of requiring evidence of an heir before the end of the year … he hadn't felt this conflicted *ever* in his long life.

With an impatient hand, he shoved through the entry to his quarters. Trosan's visage didn't immediately come to mind as it always did when he entered their apartments. Instead, it was replaced by a heart-shaped face nearly overwhelmed with hurt, wide eyes. *What was this?*

He'd turned on the human female and vented his spleen, unable to sort through the cacophony of emotions that had beset him in that chamber. And he'd caused her pain. Not the honorable pain of breaching her virginal barrier, but hurt caused by rejection and intimidation. By humiliation. He might rule this planet, and others throughout the System via his governors, but he was a sad specimen of a male to treat such a small female so.

"Ruler." Bast hovered outside the doorway. "May we speak?"

His first servant's arms were full of Lysett's discarded clothing. He'd been so mindstruck he had returned to his quarters flagrantly nude. Not that it mattered. There were no other females in his household to offend. He gestured the other man inside and dragged a robe around his body. "How is the concubine?"

"*Lady Celeste* is … fine. Perhaps taken aback by your reaction, but I believe she is fine."

"Not offended then?" *Not crushed?*

Bast looked everywhere but at him, shifting the bundle of clothing. "I … sensed … some … animosity. But I'll endeavor to explain things to her, once she … recovers her equilibrium."

Animosity? Equilibrium? "Explain."

"Master, tonight wasn't the most optimum experience, granted. Lady Celeste has done her best to prepare to assume her role as your concubine. It was perhaps a trifle—"

"Are you suggesting she has changed her mind?" Something clenched his belly, past the dissolution of his plans.

"No. No … that is, she hasn't said that precisely."

Biting off an epithet, Lysett strode past his first servant, his long strides eating up the distance toward the female Bast had chosen for him. Refusal was simply not an option. Besides her sweet and lovely appearance, she possessed admirable attributes, eminently suitable for the Ruler's concubine, and considerable time had gone into preparing her. He'd done without his first servant because he was assigned to Celeste, given the importance of this match.

Lysett would steel himself against her gamine appearance, come to terms with his unprecedented reaction to her and do his duty. As Ruler, he could be utterly convincing, and she would concede.

The breeding room was empty, save for a light, floral scent he found himself sniffing eagerly. Where was she? Turning on his heel, he made his way to his concubine's quarters. Of course, she'd retreated to her sanctuary. His steps faltered. Even as Ruler, he had no right to demand entry—but she might not be aware of that. With a measured pace, he covered the last of the distance and rapped firmly on the closed door. He felt the weight of her guard's stare upon him but ignored the male.

"Bast, I told you—" Whatever it was she'd told his first servant remained unspoken as the panel slid open and she saw him. Her wide, pretty mouth hung open before she shut it, pursing those full lips as her startlingly blue eyes narrowed.

Lowering his head briefly in greeting and to acknowledge his earlier rudeness, Lysett stepped forward. She backed away, a small figure wearing only a robe made of a clinging material that showcased her curvy body. There was no fear in her demeanor, despite the disparity in their sizes—and rank. He pushed that thought away. Thinking about such things was impractical. Rank meant little anymore, insofar as procreation went. This Celeste Raynor was more than suitable, and if he knew anything, he knew he must take responsibility for the oversight. He could *feel* her warrior influence.

"What are you doing here?" Her voice quivered with anger.

Despite his most recent thoughts of suitability and equality, he was taken aback. As Ruler, others deferred to him. At the same time, he couldn't deny that her fearless stance drew him. "I have come to speak with you."

"What? Putting me in my place earlier wasn't sufficient?"

Taking in a breath through his nose, he remained calm. "I apologize for my reaction, for the way I spoke to you. I was ... surprised by your appearance. You were not at all what I expected."

Celeste crossed her arms and he mourned the loss of observing her breasts heaving with indignation. Though the way they rested on her forearms, the nipples poking against the fabric—he dragged his attention back to the words she was hurling his way.

"And whose fault was that? If you'd taken a few minutes out of your busy schedule you could have met me in person before seeing me for the first time on that ... that bed of yours."

"The breeding pallet is tradition and—"

"And so is spending time with your chosen concubine. I've spent weeks learning your customs, both from Bast and your archives. Arranged joinings haven't been around for decades—longer. I went along with it to honor your tradition, and because it seemed important. To you."

Desperate to keep up some part of the charade and not reveal anything further, he prevaricated. "You are not a Meridian. I thought it best to revert to the old custom."

"And did the old custom involve disparaging the concubine?"

Behind the indignation and anger, Lysett detected a great deal of hurt and confusion, no surprise. It sapped his will. "It does not. And I am sorry for my reaction."

"Maybe choosing a human isn't a good idea. At least not this human." The smile she offered was painful to see and he involuntarily reached out to stroke a hand over her hair.

"It isn't you, Celeste," he murmured.

With a snort, she shoved his hand away and marched to stand by the window. "I came here in good faith, Ruler. You chose me, not the other way around. If you have issues, then I'm sorry. But you aren't making it my problem."

He most definitely had issues. He had essentially lowered a death sentence on his dearest childhood friend and fooled himself into thinking he could have meaningless couplings with an alien concubine. Contrary to his morbid thoughts, he was again sporting an enormous erection brought about by the scent and scantily covered body of the female presently defying him.

"We will take some time to familiarize ourselves with one another. Then we will attempt to further the royal line." He, who rarely compromised—or apologized—mentally congratulated himself on his calm assertion, and stared at her expectantly.

"We have a saying on Earth, Ruler. Too little too late." Her hand rose to the necklace around her slender, graceful throat, as he digested her words. "You'll have to give the next concubine a turn. I'm returning to the Dormitory staging area."

"You are refusing me?" Astonishment didn't cover the emotion deluging his body. He had bent considerably and apologized!

"I'll wait for the next offer. I have someone in mind."

Battling a ridiculous rush of jealous fury displacing everything else, including his common sense, Lysett somehow kept his temper, but all softer thoughts vanished. He didn't want to wait for another concubine and he wasn't to be denied this particular one.

Drawing on the innate power he effortlessly ruled with, he used a quiet but implacable tone. "There is no refusing the royal offer, Celeste Raynor. It is I who refuses. And I find you intrigue me, with your warrior status and spirit. You are virgin and fertile. We will learn one another and you will come to the breeding pallet in due time. And give me sons."

The shocked expression on her lovely face made him want to drag her close and kiss it away, to show her the impact she had on him. But he never shared his power. He would woo his concubine and overwhelm her with pleasure until she abandoned all thoughts of refusing his contract. She would bear his children and his House would continue. This strange draw he experienced was obviously not returned, but that was for the best. This was an arranged joining and could remain without emotion. He could manage his own with his formidable control and she could quaff the elixir.

Withdrawing, he quietly closed the door, setting the scanner to deny egress without his or Bast's permission. It was unlikely his concubine would leave his house and slip away. Where would she go that he couldn't find her? But he would avoid any hint of discord and scandal henceforth.

Chapter Six

It had been a long, sleepless night, one spent alternating between staring at that closed, locked door and tossing in her comfortable bed. Celeste couldn't put the determination in the Ruler's voice out of her head. His power had flexed visibly, and taken hers away. All her splendid umbrage, a shield of sorts against the hurt, withered in the face of the fact the man ruled the planet.

What did he even want with her? Her cheeks heated to remember his throbbing erection. His reaction to her spread-eagled nude body wasn't even real. He'd probably inhaled a bunch of that elixir, too, and was now putting the best face on it. It was more likely that he didn't want to waste all the time Bast had spent on her—and she *was* a virgin and fertile, as the Ruler had so crudely pointed out. With definite dread, she envisioned a future with a man who would do his duty while she tried to pretend he didn't excite her.

Even when he was confronting her in this very room, she'd been hard pressed to keep focused on his face and his *edicts*, when the spicy scent he exuded had curled around her other senses. And that robe… He'd been naked under it, and the fabric had slid over slabs of muscle and molded the obvious bulge at his groin. Groaning at her foolishness, she forced herself to get up. She might as well have stayed on Earth and been fooled by Roy Dupuis.

Freshening up, she chose a lightweight, long dress to slip into, over the pretty slips of cloth that Bast called ladies' underwear. Her wardrobe was now quite different from the one she and the other women had been initially allotted, and she'd be lying to say that she didn't appreciate it. The clothing and her surroundings were fit for … well, a Ruler's concubine. Too bad she hadn't measured up. With a grimace, she braided her hair out of the way and resolved to quit feeling sorry for herself.

At some point, she was going to come face to face with that man again, and there had to be a way to make him see reason and let her go. The tight feeling in her belly had to be hunger. She wasn't going to give any consideration to bad things happening if she defied him. Too far from home to seek refuge, after all. A strangled giggle slipped past her lips.

"Lady Celeste?" Bast spoke at the door, tapping the panel and disengaging the lock. "Have you risen?"

Crossing to admit him, she noted his continuing pallor and apparent anxiety. Maybe he and his master had spoken and there'd been a change of heart. "Did you come to escort me? Can I go back to the Dormitory?"

"No, Lady. My Master awaits you at the morning meal."

She didn't want to see Lysett at the table, let alone break bread—or whatever passed for that here—with him. It smacked of hospitality—and inferred her compliance. "I'd rather eat in my room."

Bast sighed. "If you won't accompany me, Master will attend you. Here."

Clenching her fists did nothing to sooth her ire, and it was pointless to take it out on Bast. Still… "You've destroyed my trust, Bast. You took advantage of my unfamiliarity with Meridia and skirted information I should have been given. He tells me I can't refuse him. What? Did you spend too much time and effort on me or something?"

The smaller man shifted and actually wrung his hands. Wetting his lips, he murmured, "I apologize, Lady Celeste. Sincerely. But he is my Ruler. Our Ruler. He has ruled and you must obey."

And just like that, Celeste's spirits sank into her shoes. He'd meant what he said, and her hopeful thoughts this morning died. Despite her efforts, tears glossed her eyes and spilled over. She dashed them away with the heel of her hand but they kept coming. Feeling powerless was conceivably the worst feeling ever. Bast had made things crystal clear—his loyalty was to his master first and foremost.

She had no family, and only a few friends here— not that they could do anything, anyhow. They were all in the process of being matched to males who kowtowed to the man she'd like to avoid. She had no home to speak of because this place was her prison. The deadline voiced by the Ruler last night was obviously the important thing, and if one pudgy Earth female's sensibilities were offended and her free will suspended, who would care? Better she'd died with her family, because where was her vaunted will to survive now?

"Lady Celeste? I regret I've distressed you. But—"

She cut him off, tired of the dance and all the pretending. "Let's get it done."

"Pardon?"

"Where are we having the morning meal?"

Bast smiled, relief softening his features and he gestured toward the stairs. "This way. Unless you'd like to freshen up first? Wash away your … tears perhaps?"

Not likely. His Ruler could take her as she came. And he'd never be her Master. Ever. She slipped past Bast and headed for breakfast, ignoring both his outstretched hand and the hurt on his face.

The Ruler lounged in an enormous chair at the head of a long table in what was clearly a dining area. She'd never eaten in the room, taking her meals in the garden or in her quarters. The air was redolent of the scent of various foodstuffs and the surface of the table was covered in dishes. Celeste had lost her appetite, but the man who rose at her entrance looked as though he could consume everything—including her. Her resolve to get things over with faltered.

"Good morn. I hope you slept well."

Ah, the pleasantries. She forced a faint smile. "Good morning."

He moved around the table to tug out a chair, and she sank into it, grateful to avoid looking at him.

As he returned to his seat, Bast hustled up to offer her a beverage close to the tea she'd once enjoyed on Earth. The Ruler watched before querying his man's intent.

"I'll try it as well. And then you're excused."

Bast threw her a glance laced with an apology that she ignored, concentrating on her 'tea'. The room seethed with silence when he departed, and she fought to keep her breathing even.

"I meant what I said last night, Celeste, though regret how … forceful I likely sounded. I am aware you are upset and also regret your tears. My choice of words was perhaps unfortunate and somewhat insensitive."

Like saying you planned to get sons from me because I met your criteria? She tried to think dispassionately and supposed if she had to have sex with someone she hadn't chosen, the Ruler would be high on the list. She felt she knew him—a little—because of Bast's education, and he was good-looking and clean. She figured he wouldn't hurt her too much because she was a valuable commodity, all trained and everything. "Sure."

He cleared his throat, but she kept her attention on her tea, formulating her words. When he offered several platters of food to choose from, she chose a slice of grain bread and a piece of fruit to pick at and move around her plate. He filled his, and once again things were quiet while they ate.

"There will be times you'll be expected to attend certain events with me, Celeste."

She started, her fork clattering against the plate. Looking just past his shoulder, so as not to have to notice his looks, she nodded. "Bast explained. He taught me your customs."

"So you know what to expect."

"Yes."

"While I appreciate the brevity of your speech, you will be required to make appropriate conversation with those invited to such events."

"Okay." She went back to crumbling the bread.

The heat of his gaze became tangible and she couldn't help lifting her own to meet it. Those green eyes were blazing and she flinched.

Instantly, the Ruler blanked his features and stared back impassively. "I understand you are unhappy with me, but we must move past that. I have asked my parents to join us for the evening meal. You should have met them before, but I…"

Celeste desperately wanted to know what he didn't say. *But I wanted to get you pregnant first? I wanted to see if you were worth it first? I wanted—* Whatever. For a guy who needed kids, he sure wasn't going about this in the right way. But of course, he was, because who had all the power here?

"If you think there's a need to meet your parents."

He stared down his aristocratic nose at her. "My mother will welcome another—that is, she'll welcome a female into our family. And she will be most helpful when you deliver."

Right. Sons. "Okay."

Clearly annoyed with her minimal engagement, he huffed, then pushed back from the table. "I will see you this evening."

It all became too much. She couldn't maintain the farce, and was desperate to get it over with. He'd do her. She'd get pregnant then he'd leave her alone until the next time. The coldness of the arrangement made her lips numb, but she spoke up. Better to get it over and done with, rather than fret and lose her mind.

"We should do the breeding pallet thing sooner than later."

The Ruler froze as he levered to his feet, his big chest hovering over the table edge, his face far too close to her own. The proximity choked the breath from her lungs, and not in a bad way. "Excuse me?"

She blinked and he sank back down. "You're going to get your own way anyhow, so I think we should get it done."

"Get it done."

He was going to make her say it, spell it out. Maybe not a real bright guy either. "Have sex, get me pregnant. I'm fertile right now, apparently, and time's a-wasting. If I catch right away, you and I won't have to see one another for a long time."

****

He'd faced all imaginable adversaries during his rule, and seen things others would never have the fortune—or misfortune—to see. And he'd heard things too, all manner of things. But those words emerging from his concubine's mouth slew him and he gritted his teeth against an unmeasured response. Part of him simply wanted to take her up on the offer, lift her from her perch on the chair, and carry her off to his rooms, where he'd introduce her to the means of getting her with child.

The cooler part of him, the one that ruled as he carried out his royal duties, warred to gain supremacy and won—marginally. He reined in his oh-so-male lust and need and regarded her dispassionately.

"That time will come, but of my choosing."

Those huge, azure eyes widened, then became awash with moisture, and her lashes dropped to hide an emotion he didn't care to decipher. The drooping of her shoulders signaled defeat and it cut him, as did her whispered response. "Okay."

He was used to the ubiquitous *as you wish, Master*. He'd noted Celeste's lack of respect in failing to append any of his titles in her conversation, of course, but had let it go in an effort to mend their differences. *Okay* and *as you wish* deferred to his will in much the same way. So why did he feel the loser?

"Celeste, if you would but open yourself to the possibility we will come to know one another and make our … joining more palatable, as well as providing a pleasant environ for my sons, I'm certain it will be for the best."

"Sure."

"See you at the evening meal, then. And Celeste? Custom requires you refer to me as Ruler. Or Master."

"Sure. Ruler."

His day was full, and he forced the memorized sight of his clearly despondent concubine to the back of his mind while he carried out his political duties. When he wasn't shifting uncomfortably in his seat as his body reminded him of the way she'd looked on the breeding pallet. And when all the information Bast had shared with such admiration wasn't popping into his head at inopportune times because he now had an actual person to apply it to.

He missed Bast. No number of assistants could

replace his first servant, but his concubine required the man's support and service. Bast had been influenced by the female as well—the man hadn't been able to hide his disapproval of the way Lysett had treated her. He hoped Celeste would forgive Bast and consider him her first servant, if not a friend.

His mother was delighted to learn of the meeting with his chosen concubine, though she'd accepted his earlier edict of consummating the relationship first. That time was of his choosing for certain, and it was flowing through his fingers like sand, but his instinct dictated that he wait for his concubine to warm to him and accept her role with grace and not glum acceptance. He could afford a week, perhaps a little better.

In the interim, he would review the reports coming in from his agents on Celeste's home world. The hints and nuggets of information had been analyzed already by Ashtun and it appeared the evidence was pointing to the heads of one or two of the opposing Houses. The *why* was curious, but not nearly as important as determining *who*, in order to snuff out the risk to his concubine and the others. The damage was already done on Earth, and for that he was sorry. There were still troops there, infiltrating the governments and endeavoring to mitigate the politics toward females, and perhaps there would be more positive social discourse between the planets in the future.

It registered that Meridia had had a great influence on that world's development, the first fairly benign as the population was left to rebuild. The second … well, that planet was now confronted with the same risk of extinction Meridia faced until infused with the hope of procreation via Earth's female inhabitants. The universe certainly worked in interesting ways.

The smaller ships tasked with delivering

compatible specimens of male humans would be arriving at Meridia in several days' time. The decision had been made to keep the genders separate, and the mother ship had transported the females, leaving the slower fighters to bring the males. The numbers were shockingly low, with the majority of Earth men refusing to relocate outright, something to do with not wishing to see their women "married off" or "whoring" to aliens. He could only hope those who did accept the offer were of a caliber suited to the remaining Meridian females.

Ashtun believed it to be true, citing open-mindedness and a lack of bigotry in those males who signed on, the self-serving males culled at the outset. He pondered the difference between the human sexes and found it fortuitous that Meridia had been blessed with locating so many human females, and that such a large number had accepted the contracts in direct contrast to the males. It hinted that Lady Celeste might soften toward him, though he might be indulging in wishful thinking. Perhaps life had been so difficult on Earth that his world was impossible to resist despite the role the females would be expected to play.

"You honor us, Celeste!" His mother was as effusive as he'd ever seen her, and even his father had unbent to welcome the new royal concubine. He'd been somewhat anxious, and thought that presenting a pregnant concubine would have more easily smoothed over the loss of Trosan, but that didn't appear to be the case. His parents welcomed her most sincerely. He struggled with the idea, the memory of his childhood friend overshadowing his earlier determination to woo Celeste.

"Uh, thank you." His concubine smiled tremulously, but she looked confused and worried.

His mother persisted, citing how fortunate

Meridia was to contract with Earth's females in order to continue their species. Reference was made to how kind and thoughtful the females were to agree to intermarry, and Celeste slowly relaxed and conversed. Except she didn't look his way, not once. Not even when he addressed her directly. She turned her head and answered, but he caught only a glimpse of long, lowered lashes and a reserved demeanor. His parents noted it too and cast him concerned looks. He cursed his own ambivalence and attempted to add to the conversation.

Ensuring his voice conveyed nothing but sincere admiration, he offered, "Celeste has applied herself with considerable diligence to her studies with Bast."

His first servant nodded and spoke to her. "You have accomplished much, Lady Celeste, and have my admiration."

"Thank you." She spoke politely to Bast but without the warmth Lysett understood she'd displayed before the breeding pallet debacle.

Now annoyed with her attitude, he spoke without thinking, he who never did so, even amongst friends and family. "My concubine has also agreed to pursue the task of begetting sons immediately, as I've made her aware of the time constraints."

Aside from a sharp gasp, Celeste made no response and his mother was too well bred to comment on his tasteless remark. Her glare more than made up for it and his father's eyes flared dark green. Bast abruptly begged for leave and exited the room without waiting to obtain it. What was wrong with him to speak thus?

"R ... Ruler is correct," his concubine murmured, studying her plate. "I agreed to come to Meridia and I signed a contract. It's not as if I had a brilliant future on Earth. And I like children."

"And you agreed to honor our son with your

acceptance," his mother said brightly, clearly making an effort to smooth things over.

He cursed inwardly at his mother's inadvertent offer of a possible avenue of escape and moved to quash it. "I have chosen, Mother, evoking the royal prerogative. The matter is closed."

She raised her eyebrows and her glare softened. He recognized that look. He recalled it from his childhood when he'd fought strenuously for something he believed in and his parent supported his belief. Patting Celeste's hand, Ellyce said, "The royal prerogative. I see. I look forward to being a grandparent, Celeste. I hope we can spend considerable time together. I'd be happy to show you around the city."

His parent's sprightly tone was an obvious attempt to lift the spirit of the room, and he once again spoiled the goodwill. How could his mother forget the risks so easily? "Celeste is confined to my home, Mother. There are dangers…"

"Of course. I'd forgotten in the excitement. I'll come here then. When I'm invited," she added hurriedly in response to Lysett's stare.

"Certainly." He forced lightness into his voice.

"I'd like that." His concubine was looking at his parents, a certain desperation tightening her lovely features. It was obvious she couldn't cope with the idea of being isolated—alone with him and without her friend, Bast.

"In the interest of me spending time with my concubine, perhaps we can close the evening," he suggested, wanting to end the awkwardness.

His parents obligingly sorted themselves and bade Celeste farewell. He resigned himself to a familial lecture and a number of questions in the future, but neither questioned him in front of his concubine. After he saw them out of the door, accompanied by their guards, he squared his shoulders and marched back to the dining area. His father's final glare and his mother's worried face pricked his conscience.

The room was vacant, the only sign of Celeste a crumpled napkin beside her empty chair. Perhaps she hadn't assimilated the rules and customs of his House as well as Bast conveyed. He strode upstairs and stopped outside the closed door to her rooms. His sense of humor, long denied, made his lips twitch. Foiled by a scrap of Earther.

Two guards merged with the shadows on either end of the hall and he composed his features before rapping sharply, wondering what he'd do if she refused to open up. Already his household was in turmoil and he'd only laid eyes on her a night ago!

The panel inched wider and Celeste's pale face came into view. She stared up at him and his hands itched to reach out, pull her close, and stroke those glorious pale tresses.

"I apologize. Sir. Ruler. I should have waited for you to dismiss me."

"Attend me."

He paced downstairs, certain she would follow, yet listening for the faint fall of her footsteps. The stuff of her dress rustled faintly and he reflected how the silvery blue material had set off her eyes and hair. So very different than the females of his planet, so different from Trosan. He was startled by the lessening of his grief as he thought about his lifelong friend and concluded she would be happy for him and his line. Guilt then pricked him as he considered he was merely seeking an excuse to forget his friend.

Taking a seat in the lounge, he watched Celeste cautiously enter the room and pause to stare at him.

"Come here." His thoughts churned and his emotions were in turmoil, but he was determined to make an effort. No goals were reached without completing objectives, after all.

She took measured steps until fetching up nearly at his feet. Reaching out, he grasped her hand and drew her down beside him. "What would you know about me?"

"Pardon?" Celeste perched on the edge of the seating, as far from him as their connected hands would allow.

"I know much about you, at least as much as you have shared in your file and your time with Bast. He believes you have been open and honest. I know your age, that you are without family, yet someone cared for yourself and survived. I know you fought bravely against odds even a seasoned warrior would avoid, that you were a leader among the other females." He went on to speak of everything he could recall. She listened, nodding and making a minute grimace on occasion but didn't voice anything. "And I wonder how it is that you weren't taken by a male on your planet."

"I didn't choose to be taken. There was no one there I wanted."

"So the necklace you wear wasn't a gift from a male courting you?"

Her little fingers flitted to caress the jewelry. "No, this was my mother's. It's all I have of her. One of your troopers was kind enough to mend the chain for me."

He knew he should respond to her loss and soothe her somehow, but was irrationally distracted by her casual reference to one of his men touching something that meant so much to her.

"Who might that have been?" He'd have Bast

make inquiries…

"Janler. I forget his House. He was the male who kidnapped me, and he was kind."

There was nothing other than sweet appreciation in her tone and Lysett forced down the reaction—that he wasn't going to identify—to another male being near his concubine. Before he'd even known of her existence.

"I'm glad he was … kind. And pleased he kidnapped you."

She blinked, surprise flickering in the depths of her eyes, and smiled tremulously. "You're likely pleased there were so many of us. Not that most wanted the men who wanted them, to my understanding."

"Do females make the choice then?" His recent reports disputed that.

"Sometimes. Sometimes not. I was fortunate to avoid having to make the choice, or concede. Until your … troopers landed."

Stroking his thumb over the soft skin of her wrist, he noted how her pulse sped up. Perhaps it wouldn't be as difficult as he thought to seduce this young female. It would definitely be kinder and set a precedent for their future. Goddess knew it would be no hard task for him personally, and he knew he was capable of keeping his distance emotionally. "And yet you accepted our offer. You didn't choose to return."

"I didn't want to—at the time."

"You wound me, Celeste. I have apologized for last night. And I offer an additional apology for my less than honorable comments this evening."

He watched her digest his words, her feelings written clearly across her face. Disbelief, caution, and tentative hope were smothered by regret. "But *I* have no choice."

"You do not." He hardened his heart against how

autocratic he sounded. Bast touted her suitability, and he, himself, desired her physically. That was enough. Arbitrarily, the thought that he might meet another concubine surfaced, and it gave him pause. His first servant would not have left anything to chance, so why was he set on this particular female?

"So how does that make it right? Or fair?" Celeste's sad, quiet voice interrupted his musings.

Carefully placing her small hand in her lap, he shifted to fully face her. "We all do things we don't always want to do or choose to do. You are aware of our females' difficulty with procreation. Bast has been most forthcoming with you in that regard?"

"Yes."

"He will not have mentioned that my first concubine died as a result of conceiving my child. Neither survived."

He wouldn't have believed Celeste's eyes could have grown any larger. He was unprepared for the sympathy that filled them and washed across her features.

"I'm sorry. I didn't know."

"My grief is private and Bast will have left it for me to share. Her name was Trosan and she was of a neighboring, high-ranking House. She was my best friend, my lifelong friend, and she did her duty as I did mine. Only it cost her life."

She swallowed and all vestiges of color leached from her face. "It's difficult to lose loved ones."

Of course, she would know the pain. She'd lost everyone and everything. Now that he'd perused her entire file, he was fully aware. He regretted his selfishness. "I see you understand. I am sorry for *your* losses."

"Is that why you didn't want to see me before last

night? Why you had Bast teach me, and avoided me until the last minute?"

"Yes." Curious how she came to such a quick understanding, but then he understood her to be highly intelligent. "*I* wasn't prepared, apparently."

"So it wasn't me. The way I looked or anything." A flush of pink inched upward from her throat and tinted her ivory cheeks.

"It wasn't about your appearance at all. In fact, I believe we are well suited. I admired the female presented before actually meeting you, and in addition, I find you ... attractive. I'm pleased Bast chose you."

"Then I think we should go through with it right away." Her small face was set in determined lines, different from her earlier challenge that they conclude the contract. He wouldn't tolerate defiance.

He was still taken aback, and thought to give her more time. "Have you nothing to ask me? Nothing you wish to talk about?"

"I trust that Bast filled me in on whatever I need to know, aside from what he obviously avoided telling me. And he couldn't because his first loyalty is to you. You've filled in the blanks."

"True, but—"

"I can't wait. I mean, I can't think about it any longer. It's too upsetting to have it out there, just waiting to happen, you know? It's like taking medicine. Best to get it done."

His pride should be punctured at being compared to medicine, but she was so earnest... And she wasn't angry or defiant. He forced a smile and found it easier than he thought. "Are you suggesting tonight?"

Flushing bright pink, she nodded. "I'm in the middle of my cycle like I said before. At my most fertile."

Contrarily, it pained him, the way his concubine stripped the situation down to the bare bones of the contract. "You may have the choice of the breeding pallet—or not."

"I don't care." She was on her feet, clenching her hands in the fabric of her skirt. Her face was pale once again and her full mouth set. "Whatever you'd prefer."

Insanely, he'd prefer to seduce and woo this scrap of female until she gave herself to him, and begged for his touch, but he had put this plan into play. And now he had no idea how to change its course without it appearing he lied about finding her attractive. Or appearing … unRuler-like. It then struck him she hadn't indicated feeling any attraction to him. Lysett had never backed down from a challenge, but he quaked in the face of this one. It didn't help that he still felt conflicted in betraying Trosan.

Working hard at hiding his quandary, he spoke in a measured voice. "Come with me."

Chapter Seven

Pattering along behind Lysett, Celeste resisted the urge to pinch herself and ensure this was real, that she was actually going to have sex with him. Instead, she focused on the tall length of him moving steadily and gracefully, the stuff of his shirt clinging to that muscled back. His long, strong legs made her take two steps to his one, and she shamelessly ogled a very nice bottom encased in form-fitting fabric that flexed as they mounted the stairs.

She should still be angry with him, but the sense of humiliation had eased with his sincere apology. Oh, she knew it wasn't a great apology, but recognized the effort—and the reasoning—behind it. As Ruler, things went his way and he'd have little call to make amends. So that made it more heartfelt in her mind, no matter it was a poor excuse for one.

Not usually given to such deep thoughts—likely because her lack of interaction with males—Celeste found herself searching behind the Ruler's public face, and thought she was correct in detecting a wealth of pain, tamped down by the effort it demanded to run his planet. Probably that was how he coped.

She felt sorry for him, easily identifying with his personal angst. Losing people one loved took its toll, and he'd lashed out at her when faced with that loss. He had a duty to perform and in all likelihood felt he was betraying his former concubine. She found that admirable even as she felt a bit like she was in competition with a ghost. Which was crazy thinking because she meant one thing, and one thing only, to him.

Analytical thoughts aside, she'd admit that she found him incredibly attractive, and surely *accommodating* his sexual overtures wouldn't be a chore. That's what she'd signed up for, so she should face facts and take the initiative, seeing as he'd evoked the royal decree that she couldn't refuse him. It gave her a modicum of power and would guard her heart in the end. One couldn't fall in love with someone if one treated the process as a clinical arrangement. And if he maltreated her, she'd tell his mother. Her anxiousness resolved, she went forward with a lighter heart. And let herself admit to a burgeoning sexual interest, manifested in the beading of her nipples and the flare of damp heat between her thighs as she anticipated what was about to transpire at his hands.

Lysett stopped at a door she remembered entering the night before, feeling both tentative and hopeful, and then fleeing out of in umbrage and confusion. Her heart hitched in her chest as he gestured her inside. Maybe sexual interest wasn't going to carry the day.

They stood facing one another, and *awkward* didn't begin to describe it. Celeste pretended the breeding pallet wasn't front and center. The Ruler smiled, the movement easing the strictness of his features and warming his eyes. He gestured, and she tracked the strength embodied in that big hand. It comforted her, somehow.

"I can order the elixir, Lady Celeste."

Someone she didn't recognize spoke from within her, in a positively teasing tone. "Will I require it?"

His green eyes darkened to a turbulent emerald, and she trembled, wishing to call the challenge back. What was she thinking? Before she could react, he was in her space, the heat of him permeating the gossamer gown she wore, and then his hands were sifting through her hair as he tilted up her head. His stare lanced to the center of her being and her belly clenched. That spicy smell wrought havoc on her senses again.

"I don't believe you'll need the elixir."

Somehow the difference in height wasn't an issue as he fit his chiseled lips over hers and worked them in soft seduction, playing against the seam until she parted to allow him access. His tongue flirted along her lower lip before skating inside in ever bolder forays, exploring her mouth and engulfing her senses with a wash of heat that made her knees fluid. He tasted of the drink they'd had at dinner and fiery male, an altogether heady mix.

As if sensing her diminishing capacity to remain upright, Lysett wrapped one arm around her and welded her to his hard chest. She stood on tiptoe and strained to get closer. His heart thundered against her breast—or maybe that was the pounding of her own. If he could reduce her to this crumbling mess with one kiss, what would his touch do? Any second thoughts she'd entertained slipped away on a river of desire.

Releasing her mouth, he trailed kisses over her cheek and temple as he set her slightly away from him, his hold firm until she was steady on her feet. She blinked until the room came into focus. The hard length of him throbbed against her abdomen and she closed her fingers into fists to resist the urge to touch. Bast had made it clear she wasn't to do so. In any event, she most definitely didn't need a drop of that elixir.

Aware he was studying her with an enigmatic look, she strained to read him. He was clearly aroused without the potion, so found her physically attractive, but there was nothing in his features or the depths of his eyes to suggest anything more than lust. No surprise, considering he was a widower of sorts and there was such a dearth of females on the planet—the man had been without female companionship for a long time. Somehow she knew he'd been faithful to … Trosan.

So what had she expected, given the circumstances of their arrangement? That he'd suddenly regard her the way her father had regarded her mother?

Shoving the romanticism aside, she huffed a tremulous breath and willed her body to cease its fine trembling. But the yearning in her core simmered with molten heat and she gave over to it, welcoming the distraction from her ridiculous thoughts. Lysett raked his gaze over her with intent and one thick brow quirked upward.

"May I undress you?"

She visualized those big hands efficiently stripping away her apparel and managed a nod. Something inside was screaming for him to go on the offensive and ravish her so she could lose herself in sensation and avoid the implication of what was about to transpire. Ambivalence threatened to derail what she'd decided was the best way to approach her current lot in life, and when his eyes narrowed, she impulsively reached to press a palm against his cheek.

His lids lowered further and a slight pressure met her hand before they sprang open, a certain coolness lightening his eyes, and she knew she'd transgressed in the effort to settle herself. His mouth set in a straight line and he stiffened. Why had she contravened the rules? What if he stopped and decided another night would suit better?

Unable to imagine the wear and tear on her nerves if forced to wait longer, she pleaded, "Please, Ruler. I don't know what to do."

Mouth softening, he set his hands on her shoulders and smoothed her gown downward, the material whispering softly against her skin as he bared her upper body. She squeezed her eyes shut, unable to observe her own seduction as the cool air made her nipples bead even tighter.

"You are lovely, Celeste. Perfect and sweet."

A press of his lips over her heart startled her eyes wide and she quivered as he went down on one knee to guide her garment over her hips and allowed it to pool at her feet. The gossamer stuff of her panties was no barrier to his avid stare and she shifted in response, that heated need between her thighs matched only by the increasing weight of her breasts.

The Ruler had a thick head of dark hair with a suggestion of curl, and she longed to weave her fingers through it, especially when he drifted his lips across her belly and along the top of her panties. But she again fisted her hands and tried to remain passive, not that she could control her breathing. She couldn't seem to fill her lungs with enough air and panted with abandon.

Hooking his thumbs in the thinner fabric at her hips, he tugged the undergarment down, where it joined her gown. One long, thick finger teased among her scant curls and Celeste wanted to kick the clothing away, freeing her feet. She didn't know if she wanted to run or step wide so Lysett had room to slip his digit between her thighs and ease the ache that continued to build.

"I scent your arousal, my sweet human."

A tiny whimper slipped past her lips at the deep and throaty tone, and any hint of embarrassment faded in the face of his appreciation, but she couldn't form any coherent response. Especially when his finger followed the seam of her cleft, sliding easily on her wetness. She wanted to press against it, and her hips hitched forward of their own volition, eliciting a pleased chuckle from the Ruler.

"Your body wants mine. This will go well, my sweet, and you'll soon bear my sons."

The reminder of their stark agreement might have

put a damper on her need, except Lysett scooped her up and placed her with infinite care on the breeding pallet. He arranged her in the same manner as that of which Bast had instructed she present herself, but this was far more intimate and harkened to a revered ceremony.

Her arms stretched wide, her palms up, Celeste noted Lysett's fervent stare as her breasts lifted and the nipples pointed higher. When his head lowered and he closed his mouth around one, lashing it with his tongue, she was nearly transported. Shivers of pleasure flowed from the site, arrowing toward the apex of her thighs, and she squirmed.

He lavished the same attention on her other straining bud, a big hand engulfing the now abandoned breast, and she moaned, a sound she'd never made before. A tiny nip made her want to thrash her head, but it remained firmly placed, and she was forced to endure the pleasurably painful suckling.

Releasing her nipple at last, Lysett blew across it and she sucked in a draught of air, trying to collect herself as he traced her rib cage and then her hips with his fingertips. "You are not so tall, Celeste," he murmured. "I should splay your legs wide and place them firmly. But I find I wish them set just so."

Bending each knee, lightly gripping her calves, he eased her thighs apart and she too could scent her tart aroma of her need. Her toes danced across the surface of the pallet and remained free of its hold. Willing herself to relax and trust him to arrange her body, she watched as he studied her sex.

Those green eyes flared hotter, and glittered, causing her to dampen further while her heart rate increased and fluttered in the hollow of her throat. Everything felt sharper and incredibly intimate and she desperately held to the passion overwhelming her, refusing to acknowledge any softer emotions.

"Are you all right?" His gaze shifted to engage her own.

She didn't want to talk, didn't want to categorize or label what was transpiring. This was about honoring the contract and nothing further. She wouldn't misinterpret anything encompassed within that green stare, intuitively knowing better. "I'm okay," she whispered.

"I wish to taste you and ensure you are ready to take my seed."

Uncertain what one had to do with the other, she managed a shaky nod and sucked in another shuddering breath when that dark head descended between her legs and he pressed a kiss against her inner thigh. Somehow her feet became draped over his shoulders and she shamelessly accepted the teasing flicks of his tongue as they lanced between her nether lips.

In fact, she offered herself willingly, arching into his expert ministrations, while her torso remained immobilized. The tingling sensation built in a wavering circle from her navel to her quivering thighs. He cupped her buttocks, lifting her higher still. When he worried the knot of nerves at the top of her apex, the tingling coalesced into one stunning burst of rippling sensation. Incoherent words and high-pitched cries echoed in the aftermath and she realized it was her making those sounds.

Lysett lifted his head, the lower part of his face shiny and wet, and gifted her with a smile she couldn't help but accept and tuck away to remember later. To recall and examine with a brain not mushy from such intense pleasure.

Levering to his feet, he stripped off his clothes as efficiently as the previous night, but this time, she detected no anger or regret. She rested her feet lightly against the pallet, knees negligently spread and wondered at her lack of modesty. Was this what feminine power felt like? Certainly Lysett appeared enthralled, and while she'd be nothing more to him than a broodmare, she could clasp this moment—and any that might follow—as a talisman against future regrets. She knew there would be those dark times ahead, but she wasn't thinking about that now.

Not when there was a beautiful male specimen looming over her, one capable of bestowing physical pleasure and granting her a safe and prosperous position in his household as she raised precious children. The part of him that signified his utter maleness evoked a tremor of fear, but she trusted him not to hurt her past the breaching of her virginal barrier. His cock stood proudly to the tempting 'V' of his abdomen, reaching toward his navel, broad and wide at the head. She reminded herself once again that women accommodated men since the beginning of time and swallowed her worry.

"I'll take care with you, Celeste." Had he read her concern? Regardless, his look was tender and she smiled, this time easily.

"I believe you."

Making a place for himself between her thighs, she felt the hard, velvety length of him split her cleft, and she eased her knees wider around his hips to cradle him against her pelvis. She wished she could lift her arms to hold him closer, but intuited that attempt at closeness would be received in the same manner as her touch on his cheek. Instead of tightening her legs, she reminded herself to remain passive and accepting.

He inserted a hand between them and guided his cock to her opening, a natural and unerring movement that spoke to his experience, and the head worked past the initial stricture a fraction. She tensed despite herself.

"There's no help for it the first time, my concubine." The label felt like an endearment and she made a brave smile. A hard thrust followed and she bit her lip against the sharp pain and too-full sensation as he filled her.

Stilling, he gave her time to adjust, watching her carefully, even as his face showed considerable strain. The skin stretched tightly over his cheekbones and his mouth set tightly as he waited. She drew in and released considerable amounts of air through her nostrils, trying not to second-guess her decision. It was too late, anyhow, and she cautiously squeezed around his girth.

"Goddess, don't do that." Lysett audibly ground his teeth and that hint of feminine power returned. She might have accepted him into her body, but he clearly found it to be a pleasurable experience and one that she alone could give him if, as Ruler, he honored monogamy. She clenched harder, and he responded by pulling away, then pushing forward until a certain rhythm developed.

She rocked to meet him and in sync, their movements sped up. Lysett slammed his hands down on either side of her face and his own was a study of intense concentration and what had to be burgeoning pleasure. The green of his eyes intensified as the pupils dilated to absorb the grassy color, and she allowed herself to forget her role, just for the moment. Her discomfort abated and she could admit to a different kind of pressure, one similar to the tingling that had built into that exciting, earlier blossom of climax.

With a groan, he shoved deep and held himself hard against her, a shudder overtaking his strong body as her channel tightened and loosened in a warm ease of tension. A different sensation but entirely satisfying, and one that made her glow.

Lysett lowered his chest to brush her tender nipples and a guttural sound filled her ears as he shoved his face against her neck and his breathing slowed. A fine dew of sweat cooled between them and she knew she'd never forget this first time.

Then the Ruler disengaged, and not just physically, although his cock slipped free and wet heat anointed her thighs. She focused on that wetness, hoping a child had been conceived, rather than acknowledge his emotional withdrawal. He had done his duty and was now removing himself from the equation. Stupid, but she was crushed.

A novice, she still craved something … more. His proximity maybe, and a press of his skin. Perhaps another kiss.

He stood, and hovered awkwardly beside the pallet. The look didn't suit him.

"I'll fetch you a cleansing cloth, Celeste."

The sight of his perfect, naked form retreating from her was distraction enough. The thought of another such encounter with him before she rebuilt her defenses would sorely test her resolve to keep their connection superficial. Celeste had just learned an important fact about herself and she somehow held the accompanying tears at bay. Casual coitus wasn't for her, so she had to hope she could limit that physical interaction with Lysett by early conception. Or risk a relationship that was one-sided and certain to cause her great pain.

****

Hurriedly cleaning himself, Lysett studiously avoided his reflection as diligently as he avoided thinking about what had just transpired. It was enough he'd been able to seduce his concubine, give her great pleasure and hopefully make a child with her. The attraction had overwhelmed him and their coupling was magnificent. He swallowed a groan at the memory of her silky skin beneath him and the sweet clasp of her body around his cock. Even now he wanted to have her again. And again. It was that certain other something that poked at him and was so unsettling. One hand drifted uncertainly upward to touch his face where her small hand had pressed in the midst of his turbulent thoughts, somehow pushing past to reach him as if forging a connection...

But he wasn't thinking about that. Surely Trosan held that piece of him, whatever it was, and he would never betray her memory. Celeste had served him sweetly and well, and he would treat her accordingly, but she would never gain the stature his childhood friend had occupied. And he was damned if he'd feel remorseful about it. His concubine would be well cared for and lack nothing. He would raise fine sons and perhaps daughters with Celeste and further his House. Meridia would benefit and his race wouldn't die out because others would also procreate.

Making his way back to his concubine, he made every attempt to view what they'd engaged in as clinically as possible while exuding kindness. Strange that he felt neither. Oh, there was a certain tenderness in his regard for Celeste, but aside from that raging need to have her again, he had to fight against that *something*. And it wasn't kindness—that was too tame. It made him annoyed and she winced when he stared at her.

Quickly composing his features, he forced a smile and reached to cleanse her thighs and pretty pink parts. His cock had sported the evidence of the loss of her virginal barrier, and he suspected she would be tender.

"That's okay. If you'd release me, I'll clean up myself." Her request was fraught with anxiousness and her big, blue eyes pleaded with him.

"I would take care of you," he offered.

"Unless it's part of the … process, I wish you wouldn't." Her voice had firmed and she struggled to raise her arms and lift her head. Her obvious distaste for any further touch made his smile feel brittle. But seeing as it was precisely what he wanted, a coupling during her fertile periods, he could hardly take umbrage.

Pressing on strategic points of the pallet, he released Celeste and helped her to her feet, noting how she swiftly put space between them. He tried to pay no heed to the strange slice of pain her action caused, and offered the cloth. She nearly snatched it from him and walked gingerly toward the cleansing room, any suggestion of her confident demeanor long past, though her full buttocks moved enticingly before his appraising stare. Well, it was to be expected, this awkwardness. They hardly knew one another and the joining was a political necessity. Virginal Celeste was hardly the type of female who would know how to comport herself after a physical encounter.

The idea of her having such encounters with anyone other than himself lit a fire in his belly and he rubbed the area to ease it. Useless imaginings when fidelity was their watchword going forward. It occurred that their joinings could well be confined to once every year or so if Celeste was as fertile as predicted, and he could find scant comfort in that fact. With a grimace, he decided his heart and his cock had entirely different agendas, and searched for the guilt and shame to douse the latter. It was disconcerting that he was unable to muster up any.

"I'd like to return to my space." His concubine stood nearby, having returned on silent feet. Her attention was focused on her hands, twisting in the fabric of the gown she'd donned, hiding what he deemed was his. It was a real effort not to demand she remove it, and a stronger one not to advise she would now share his quarters. He rubbed his forehead and decided to remove himself from her presence before she further adversely affected him.

Stepping into his pants, he fastened them and snatched up his shirt. "I'll escort you."

"Thank you." She preceded him and didn't glance upward at all. He gazed down at the disheveled mass of her pale hair and wished he might smooth the tangled locks. A chilly, polite distance grew between them and he told himself welcomed it.

After a few more strides, they gained her door, and he held it open while she passed through. He searched for something to say, some words that would reflect the acumen he displayed in the political forums, but nothing surfaced.

She spoke through the narrow aperture as it closed, "I will know if we require a medical confirmation of tonight... That is, if it was successful, in twelve to fourteen days, Ruler."

The smooth panel was a direct contrast to his roiling thoughts as he bleakly stared at it, hearing no movement beyond to suggest that his concubine was even present. He touched his fingertips to the surface and pressed his palm flat as he accepted he'd reduced this part of his life—and hers—to the occasional passionate coupling as a means to an end. It left a bad taste in his mouth, especially when he wondered if the passion would wither and die without nurture.

Morat's big form lingered at the far end of the hall, carrying out his orders to keep Celeste safe, something Lysett wished he could do personally, insofar as his concubine's tender spirit went.

He made his way to his quarters, the distance

suddenly interminable as weariness overtook him. Not the welcome tiredness following a lustful coupling as he recalled from the distant past, but one he might attribute to his conflicted feelings—if he could but admit to them. In that moment he decided not to call in his healer to test Celeste for conception, there being no need to wait for her timeline, considering their advanced technology. He could wait a few days, and perhaps offer his concubine a little time to acclimate.

Chapter Eight

Celeste huddled beneath the covers and stared at the ceiling through gritty eyes. Her bed was scant comfort, but she thought she might keep taking to it in an effort to avoid her life. Sleep had been long in coming, and then fractured by snippets of erotic dreams that ended the same way, with Lysett abandoning her after making a strenuous—and extremely pleasurable—effort to beget a child with her. She made an experimental stretch and, aside from a slight soreness between her legs, decided she felt okay physically.

Feeling a hot bath was in order, she threw back the bedding and swiveled her feet to the floor, sitting up to view the space—her lovely prison cell—with a resigned stare. Making her way to the cleansing room, she allowed the light nightgown to slip off and stared at her nude form in the mirror. She looked no different after her deflowering, then realized her face was set in a neutral cast, her eyes blank. Forcing her lips upward in a smile, she accepted the action didn't do much to improve her appearance.

Soaking in the tub, her hair piled on top of her head, she reflected on the coming days and weeks. The years. If she let herself perseverate about the male she'd contracted with, and narrowed her life to the occasional 'events' she would attend with him, and the rarer moments in pursuit of conceiving a child, she'd likely be as crazy as those poor, brainwashed women back on Earth. Though if enough time elapsed between those efforts at conception, she'd hopefully forget the way he'd unleashed her sexuality and cease to long for it.

She'd never given up easily, and realistically, her lot here was far better than it had been back home, so she needed to get a grip and deal. She'd been spending far too much time thinking about the same issues over and over. Now the deed was done, she would make the best of things. Starting with getting out and about. She wanted to see Shirley and a few other women she'd come to know. She needed to find something useful to do, now that her studies—and the main event—were concluded.

After washing herself and drying off, she carefully chose a dress suitable for the day. She stared longingly at her boots, set neatly side by side in the closet, but Bast had ideas about what a royal concubine should wear, so that was a battle for another time. She had other, far more important things to deal with today. Ruthlessly braiding her hair, coiling it around her head, she affixed it tightly with some lovely jeweled pins the Ruler's mother had gifted her. Her mom's necklace looked so simple in contrast, so she tucked it into the bodice of her dress as a reminder of who she truly was beneath the trappings. Without another glance at her appearance, she stepped to the door and opened it. Instantly, her guard—Morat—was there.

"Lady Celeste?"

"I'd like to go to breakfast."

With a deferential nod, he gestured her ahead, and she went down the stairs to the eating area. The room was empty, the huge table set with two place settings, and despite her resolve not to allow any hint of anticipation or hope, she wondered if Lysett would be joining her. It might be best to get that awkward day-after moment behind them. If she became overcome with a need to indulge with him again and couldn't hide it, he could reject her and crush such stupidity.

"You have risen." Bast's cheerful voice sounded behind her and he pressed past Morat. "I hoped to take the morning meal with you."

She still wasn't feeling charitable toward the Ruler's first servant, and ridiculous disappointment nearly flavored her response. But if she was going to accomplish any of her goals, it was best to have him onside. "Good morning."

He studied her face intently before a faint flush stained his cheeks. "Good morning. Are you … well?"

Did she look so different? "I'm fine."

With an inner shrug, she went to a place setting and Bast hustled to hold the chair. Thanking him, she settled herself and kept her composure. It didn't take much effort, all her emotions once again contained and quiescent, or so she assured herself. Bast took his place and fidgeted with a utensil.

The young serving male entered with a large tray and deposited it in front of them, and Bast hurriedly offered her a plate of fruit. She chose a few pieces and accepted a slice of her favorite bread, declining the protein substitute.

"You must eat a balanced diet," he chided.

Ah, so he knew the deed was done. Of course, he did. His Master probably had him enter it in a journal, or tick it off on a ledger line. *Had sex with the royal concubine. Match concluded.* Now Bast's biggest priority would be to ensure the impending royal fetus received only the best nutrition. Celeste decided to be bitchy. "What's the importance of a balanced diet?"

Bast's stare danced away from hers and found his plate interesting. His cheeks flushed again and his shoulders hunched. She indulged in petty delight in his discomfort before cutting him some slack. She speared the protein and dumped it on her plate beside the fruit.

They ate in silence for a few minutes, before he broke it. "Today, Lady Celeste, I thought perhaps—"

Lord, he was going to tutor her again, or something.

Maybe lecture her on being a mom-in-waiting. Nope. She cut him off.

"I want to visit Shirley."

"I would need to speak with our Master—"

"Then do so. And while you're at it, please get permission for me to attend the market with his mother. I want to purchase items for the garden. I need to be outside." She had no idea if she could ask for whatever passed for money on Meridia but assumed being the Ruler's concubine meant she would be allotted some.

Swallowing, Bast nodded, still avoiding her eyes. He patted his mouth with a napkin and stood, offering the same deferential nod her guard had given. "Please finish your meal, Lady Celeste. I'll return shortly." Maybe his ever-present screen wasn't on his person.

"Thank you." She regretted her imperious manner, but if it was the means to carving out a life for herself here, she'd use it when she had to.

She had cleaned her plate and indulged in a second glass of juice when he returned, looking anxious. Probably caught between his implacable master and what he expected to be a petulant concubine.

"The Ruler will not give permission for you to attend the market, I'm afraid. Though you may, of course, spend time in the garden, and Shirley will be escorted here to visit."

"If you'd loan me your screen, perhaps I might discuss attending the market with your master." She hadn't really expected permission to go, recalling the discussion with his mother, but wanted to see Lysett's face. Stupid, but there it was. Surely she had the right to make eye contact with the man who'd taken her virginity and proclaimed her his concubine without any recourse.

"Ah, the Ruler is here, Lady. In his office. Here. I spoke with him personally."

She pushed to her feet. "Then I'll ask him personally."

"He isn't to be disturbed." Bast's face was as stone, all earlier emotions vanished, and she got the message. The Ruler only had time for her on … certain occasions.

"Of course. Another royal edict I wasn't aware of—or forgotten." She managed the words with absolutely no inflection and plastered a cool smile on her own face. "Thank you, Bast. I'll be in the garden. When Shirley arrives, please ask her back."

He might have replied, but she was on the move, so quickly that Morat was visibly startled as he caught up. She wrestled the figurative slap in the face of Lysett's snub into submission, and tucked it away, not wanting her guard to see her reaction and draw any conclusions. They were joined by a second guard, someone unfamiliar but as obsequious, and she entered the walled garden with vast relief.

There were other males on the perimeter, easily ignored, as they blended into the shadows, and she knew they were there for her protection. The day was already warm, but the foliage shielded her from the sun and the flower bed she headed toward was well in the shade. She sank down on the edge and began the mindless task of weeding the strange blossoms.

As she worked, the soothing feel and scent of the plants surrounding her, she thought about anything and anyone other than Lysett. She wondered how the other concubines were faring and allowed herself a few sad moments of thinking about Lauren. The older woman was likely aware Celeste was one of the kidnapped and would no doubt have been terribly upset. She hoped the Meridians still on Earth were successful in protecting the women who had been returned. Maybe Bast could get a message to Lauren...

"Lady Celeste?" Bast spoke quietly off to her left.

With a grimace, she straightened to face him. How long had she been on her knees? A massive pile of weeds and a stiff body suggested a considerable length of time. "Yes, Bast?"

"Lady Shirley is on her way. I thought perhaps you'd like to freshen up and have something to eat?"

Looking at her dirty hands, she nodded. She probably had dirt on her face too, from where she'd swiped at loose tendrils of hair sticking to her forehead and cheeks. "I'll come in right away. Thank you."

He came closer and offered his hand.

Waving it away, she clambered to her feet. He didn't hide his hurt, and she hastened to explain. "No point in getting you dirty, too, Bast. But thanks, anyway."

"We have gardeners for weeding," he said.

She wasn't giving in, not about this, not even if her missing-in-action Ruler said so. "I need something to occupy myself. I love to grow things, nurture them. And if I can't leave the premises until the risk to me has diminished, I'll garden. Procreating won't fill all my time."

"I'm sorry, Lady Celeste. I truly am."

"For what?" She wasn't being snarky now. And it was time she forgave the man. He'd only been doing his job after all, and believed what he'd been doing was right for an entire planet. It was clear he didn't approve of the way his master treated her, his loyalty shifting a little. In addition, she was desperate for a friend of any sort.

"For ... everything." He threw up his hands, a most surprising action for such a learned and composed servant.

"I've accepted my lot," she said briskly. "You

needn't apologize again, and certainly not on behalf of your master. But I'd appreciate your support in helping me keep … occupied. I seem to have no idea what a concubine is allowed, or not allowed, to do when I'm not…"

Abruptly realizing this was, in all likelihood, Trosan's garden, she blanched. Leaning forward, she whispered. "Am I allowed to work out here? Was this place hers?"

Stark pain lanced through Bast's eyes and tightened his lips. Celeste recognized more than one male in this house had loved the deceased concubine and her heart shriveled. She'd ever be a reminder of what had been and would be no longer, and a surge of hopelessness made her sag.

Bast lightly grasped her arm and she welcomed the support. "Lady Trosan's interest wasn't in plantings. She helped our Master with political issues and the like. The garden was planted by Lady Ellyce and the gardener comes but once a month to tend it. You must think of it as your own."

Of course, Trosan helped Lysett with intellectual matters. She'd been Meridian, after all, and of a high House. It put Celeste more firmly in her secondary role, but she quashed the resentment. The other woman had died, trying to give her Ruler a child, and if Lysett and Bast worshiped her, it should come as no surprise. Celeste really needed to grow up and deal.

"I'll do that. Thank you." She'd kill everyone with kindness from here on out and hide her heart more fiercely.

With a sweet smile, Bast set her grubby hand on his arm and escorted her inside. She walked beside him with her head held high, apeing her betters and resolving to fool everyone, even herself.

****

Lysett drew back from the window and hurried to exit his concubine's room and gain his office before she found him loitering. He'd watched her toiling in the garden for hours, crouched beside the flowers, the skirt of her gown feathered out around her. The gold of her hair seemed subdued, confined as it was to the shape of her delicate skull. He wished she'd left it to flow over her shoulders and down the length of her back, but supposed she'd arranged it to stay out of the way while she worked.

His mother found tending the flowers peaceful and relaxing, and Celeste no doubt was chafing at her necessary house arrest. His forehead pressed up against the cool pane as his brain whirled with mixed thoughts and emotions. Perhaps he could escort her to the marketplace, and have his parents attend, or even his mother… With a grimace, he sought to order his thoughts.

He'd chosen not to see her at the morning meal, citing work obligations to Bast, though he hadn't been able to make himself attend his government office. He'd told himself it was because of her final words to him the previous evening, the ones spoken through the gap of the closing door, her azure eyes wide and full of hurt and bewilderment. There was no reason to spend time with her outside of certain functions and of course those times to sire an heir. The sooner they both accepted the roles they were to play, the better. So why did he badly want to lay eyes on her and spend time in her presence? He was actually thinking of taking her shopping! And if he was honest with himself, he'd entertained another session or two on the breeding pallet, before calling in the healer. He was a selfish boor, but he ignored the revelation.

Her quarters smelled of her, that singular floral

essence he'd now recognize anywhere, and after refusing to allow her to attend the market without the fortitude to do it in person, he had made his way here. Standing in a place infused with her, watching her from above, was a poor substitute, but all he'd grant himself in his ambivalence. With a grimace, he hardened his heart yet again.

Lady Celeste was no replacement for Trosan. She might be best considered a surrogate and he'd not give her reason to think outside her station. Gaining his private space, he sat at his desk and considered the work he'd avoided. As soon as Lady Shirley arrived and the two females were occupied, he would make his way to his government office and attend to pressing issues.

"Master?" Bast had slipped in without him knowing, and Lysett started. This too was another example of how distracted he'd become, an altogether unhealthy attitude considering the dangers brewing with this ridiculous purist hype presently afoot.

"Yes?"

"Am I to remain here for the day?"

"No. You can accompany me. We are lagging behind and I have granted audiences this afternoon." He hoped he gave an indication about who he held responsible for that lagging, and immediately was ashamed of himself. He'd always been a fair ruler, or so he hoped, and neither Bast nor his concubine should take the blame for his own issues.

"Of course." Bast bowed his head but didn't look at him.

"Lady Celeste is settled for the day?" He hadn't meant to ask, but the question slipped out.

"She is. Her visitor has arrived and I expect they'll be together for the remainder of the afternoon. I wondered if I should tell your concubine you'd take the evening meal with her."

"No. But inform her of the upcoming presentation. She is to dress accordingly. All eyes will be on us."

Bast's disapproval was palpable, but he said nothing other than to indicate he'd carry out his Master's wishes. Lysett ignored his first servant's body language and stalked from his home. It was best he avoided her. There was only a week before the presentation. Ashtun would surely have found the dissenters by then. He didn't think about what it would be like to be hand in hand with his concubine, touching her publicly to reassure his supporters of their righteous connection while deterring the detractors. Celeste's gamine appearance would silence critiques who would compare her to Trosan, and he would treat her as the treasure she was. In public. And if the Goddess was willing, she was already with child. He'd send for a healer—tomorrow.

Chapter Nine

"This place is amazing." Shirley gawked and paused to stroke a frieze on the wall. "The Commander and I have a nice home, but this is … well, it's royal."

"Lysett *is* the Ruler." Celeste ushered her friend down the hall to the living area. The heat of the day was upon them but that room, especially, would be light and airy with its high windows so cleverly placed to catch the breezes.

"And what's it like to be the royal concubine?" Shirley plunked herself down on a chair and tucked her feet up. She looked vibrant—happy and content, yet brimming with enthusiasm.

"It's fine." Celeste tried to infuse her voice with sincerity. It *was* fine. She lacked for nothing. Except for a male who saw her as more than a broodmare. And it was ridiculous to feel hurt because she'd known what she was signing up for…

All the animation drained from her friend's face and she leaned forward. "Fine? That sounds like … nothing. Aren't you being treated well? You look well. You've gained some weight and you're dressed beautifully."

"I'm—"

"Bullshit. I was so busy being overwhelmed by this house and how swanky you look that I didn't see *you*. We might not know one another very well, but you're not you. What's wrong?"

"Shirley. I'm fine. Seriously." She waved her hand at her surroundings, mimicking her friend. "I made this trip here, to Meridia, like everyone else, knowing the end result. I'm matched with a handsome, powerful male and I have everything I didn't have on Earth. But I'm really glad you came because I was getting lonely."

"Oh. Okay. I guess it's been awhile. You haven't seen any of the others?"

"No. I had extensive studies before I could be matched. I mean, I was chosen, but he's the Ruler and all…"

Folding her arms, Shirley tilted her head. "So the process was different?"

Desperate to find out what *process* the other woman experienced, Celeste nodded and smiled brightly. "I understand it's different."

"Because he's the Ruler and *all*. I guess that makes sense. Once Adares offered for—chose—me, we spent a little time together. But I already had my mind made up." Shirley winked and Celeste smiled harder. "Let's just say I didn't refuse and we consummated our agreement. Right away."

"It looks like, uh, things agree with you."

"They do indeed. I think I'm already pregnant." She glowed and hugged herself. "I have to see a medico—a healer—tomorrow, but I'm pretty sure. Adares is over the moon."

"That's wonderful!" She meant it. She was thrilled for her friend and her male. Before Shirley could inquire as to her status, Celeste asked about the other women they both knew.

"I've heard most of the matches are going well. Some women refused and returned to their dorms but will have meetings with different males. I think pretty much everyone has been lucky out of the group we were in, but it's early days. Belinda has met someone pretty special, though, a Liaison Ashtun. He's a big wig." She rattled off a few other names. "Wouldn't your … wouldn't the Ruler know better than me?"

Shirley didn't know any more than she did, and

Celeste had listened when Bast had shared. But it was nice to have confirmation. "I heard similar stories."

"That's good then. It looks like the Meridians meant it when they told us we would be treated well and properly matched. I had my doubts at first, but then the Commander offered for me."

Celeste didn't mention the role she'd played in that happenstance. Instead, she moved the conversation on, before Shirley asked intimate questions she didn't want to address. "I hope that once the dissent dies down a bunch of us can get together."

Her friend sobered. "Adares is worried, too. It doesn't sound like a big movement, but those with concubines are on guard and those loyal to them are helping with precautions. I heard there are rumblings about purges, that the purists would rather see Earth females eradicated and risk their species' extinction."

It chilled her blood to think of it. "I know the Ruler is concerned. I'm confined to this house."

"Not unexpected. You are the royal concubine, and if anything happened to you…"

Lysett would have to choose another, and if so many were already matched… Celeste better understood his rationale about her safety but didn't enlighten Shirley. "He's certainly taken precautions. And now I feel guilty about asking to see you!"

Shirley chuckled. "I came disguised if you recall. I'm as tall as a Meridian female, or almost, and in this outfit and the cloak, accompanied by only one male, who'd be the wiser?"

"With only one guard?" Horrified, Celeste shoved to her feet. "What was the Commander thinking? This residence is bound to be under scrutiny."

"Oh, he wasn't far, honey. Him and a bunch of his men. But hiding in plain sight is best. Relax."

And Shirley's male could hardly turn down the summons from his Ruler for his concubine to visit. Celeste felt sick. Sick and selfish. "I shouldn't have asked for you."

"Nonsense. I'm happy you did. And we can use their communication systems now, right? Have a gossip every day. Maybe Belinda can be included and some of the others."

Now that she was officially the Ruler's concubine in every sense, she supposed the communication restriction could be lifted, so she nodded at her friend. "For sure. I'll ask. It'll be safer."

They chatted about everything and anything they'd learned about Meridia, from the societal rules to fashion, avoiding politics by mutual accord. Shirley, too, had a mother-in-law if that was the right terminology. She wasn't enthralled, confiding the older woman had pressured her and Adares to live in the family home and wasn't pleased when Shirley hadn't fallen into line. They laughed at the similarities to Earth males and their mothers.

While enjoying the light repast served by the same young male, Shirley asked if Celeste was required to wear something special denoting her station at the upcoming presentation.

Morat stepped inside, his bulk drawing the eye, and saving her from admitting she had no idea what her friend was talking about. "Lady Shirley should be leaving soon. Perhaps immediately after the refreshments. The Commander has made contact."

Shirley instantly set her cup down. "I'm ready."

Flustered by this *presentation* and amused by the other woman's obvious desire to see her male, Celeste got up and hugged her friend. "Thank you for coming."

"I'll see you next week. And I'll have news for

you then! Maybe you'll have some for me?"

Somehow she'd escaped being grilled about her relationship with the Ruler, and Celeste's relief made her knees weak. She was happy for her friend, and not at all envious. There were likely a number of other matches similar to her own, with women settling, and being grateful for their lot, right? Shirley would see everyone's match through her own happy lenses. Celeste's past circumstances weren't wonderful, but many others had been far grimmer, to judge by the stories shared on the trip here. So for sure women would settle, as she had. It was almost laughable, considering how others would perceive her luck.

"I'll look forward to next week." Once she found out what it was.

Shirley donned her cape and swirled the hood over her head. With her features covered, and in native garb, she didn't look any different than the few Meridian females Celeste had observed, so she breathed easier. A tall warrior escorted her out and Celeste watched until the pair climbed into a small conveyance that powered off almost immediately. Several others followed within the space of several minutes, and she supposed those were the extra guards. The Commander was probably in the one Shirley had boarded.

With a sigh, she turned back into the house and headed up the stairs to her room. It had been good to see Shirley, but stressful too because she couldn't confide in her friend. Hers wasn't a love match, not even a hint of romance imbued it, and she didn't want any pity. Or to worry her friend. She also wanted to protect the Ruler's privacy, her studies not being lost on her. Bast would be proud. And when she next saw that male, he'd darn well explain this upcoming presentation to her.

****

"Report." It was distasteful to have his first servant bring him up to date on his concubine in the same way he was apprised of everything else of importance, but he felt he had no other option. If he spent time with her, she'd get increasingly under his skin in that indefinable way she had.

"Lady Celeste had a pleasing visit with her friend, Sir, and the guards advised there was nothing untoward in Lady Shirley's arrival or departure. I would expect your residence is being monitored, but no one is obvious, so it will be from a distance."

He wondered what the females had spoken about but quashed his curiosity. "Have you advised her of the presentation?"

"Your concubine was already aware, Master." Bast winced, before schooling his features. "I don't believe she was happy to learn it from Lady Shirley."

"She was harsh with you?" His concubine must learn to control her reactions and show a controlled demeanor in public, although he accepted it wouldn't necessarily be the same with his immediate staff. And him, if he allowed himself to spend time with her.

"No." Bast hesitated and clearly chose his words. "She was angry with me at first for … well, for circumstances surrounding the first time you and she met, and this morning there was some coolness, but… I mean to say, she struggled with the lack of information."

"Struggled?" He shouldn't feel a pang of guilt. But his first servant was obviously pained.

"She was hurt—and likely humiliated—to not be apprised of events involving her. But when I explained you had only just scheduled it, she accepted."

He'd chosen the date immediately after consummating the joining with Celeste. But then he hadn't deigned to see her at the morning meal…

Bringing his thoughts up short, he quit castigating himself. Celeste shouldn't take umbrage. He said as much to his first servant.

"Indeed, Sir. Though I confess she actually accepted it as if she deserved nothing better. I find myself unsettled and dismayed, Master. The wonderful young female I prepared to be your concubine is fast becoming distant."

It was easier to be angry than allow himself to fall prey to the surge of other emotions he preferred not to label. "Considering the stellar attributes you ascertained when you considered Lady Celeste, resilience being one of them, I'm certain she will manage, Bast. You were responsible for her education yourself, were you not? Do you doubt her suitability?"

Bast bowed low, depriving Lysett of a view of his face. His tone reflected nothing other than subservience. "I do not, Master."

"Then what is your concern? I will have a suitable royal concubine and sons to continue my house. Meridia will continue."

His first servant straightened and faced him. "And you might have had happiness, Master. And the Lady Celeste as well."

A fist gripped his heart and another his throat. He hadn't raised a hand to a servant—ever. There had never been a need. He wanted to tell Bast that his loyalty was in doubt and reassign him. Perhaps as Celeste's permanent personal assistant, seeing as the man was so concerned about her wellbeing. Or somewhere *distant*, where he needn't hear the subtle—and not so subtle—chiding. His first servant had become too familiar.

But Lysett knew himself well and breathed through his reaction, managing his rage. If Bast's words were meaningless, Lysett would have found it within himself to scoff and dismiss them. Instead, he'd struggled and initially hid behind a visceral reaction. He'd been there before, as a younger man, challenged during his fight to gain his station, and had learned from it.

"Leave me, Bast. Tend to Lady Celeste and reassure her to your best ability. We must all learn to live within our roles and remember our station."

"Sir." Bast backed out of the room, again displaying a subservience that reflected a much earlier time and Lysett nearly flinched. But he'd set his course and wouldn't deviate. A Ruler had no time for inner conflict and he was finished with second-guessing himself. He longed for Trosan's counsel, though suspected she too would offer something he wasn't prepared to hear.

It was the end of the day, so he contacted Ashtun and was astonished at the visible change in his friend and ally. Had the man sought rejuvenating treatments? The Liaison's features were definitely no longer strained and while his shoulders were still squared and his posture erect as befitted his military background, there was a certain jauntiness to his demeanor.

"Ruler. I wish I had better news." A hint of strain etched the other man's handsome face as he spoke, but didn't mar his obvious happiness. "I have no evidence, merely speculation. I believe the dissent is confined and not growing as rapidly as first predicted. I remain fixed on two Houses, but no additional evidence has been compiled. But it is still a concern."

"You look well, my friend." Lysett dismissed the unfavorable report. They couldn't proceed without evidence and Ashtun was diligent—and vigilant.

"I am, Sir. My concubine has accepted my contract and enriches my life already. My gratitude knows no bounds. Which is why I am additionally encouraged to find the source of this purist movement and deal with it. Nothing must threaten Meridia's future."

"I am happy for you. And I most certainly have faith."

Ashtun nodded. "I'll advise you as soon as I know anything further. Ruler, how is the royal concubine? My concubine and I look forward to meeting her. They know one another, from the ship."

"Lady Celeste is … an extremely suitable royal concubine. You'll be one of the first to meet her at the presentation. I'm sure she'll be pleased to see an old friend."

Closing the connection, he thought to order a meal sent to his quarters, then changed his mind and decided to dine with Celeste and Bast. There were some bridges to be mended if those attending the upcoming event were to be convinced of her suitability. Bast could diligently prepare her, but the social discourse between Celeste and Lysett would be under scrutiny. He owed it to her to work on their familiarity with one another, or so he told himself.

After changing into more comfortable attire, he made his way to the dining area. The room was empty, and there was no sign of place settings. Frowning, he called for Vorst. The young serving male hastened to the room.

"Master?"

"Why is there no evening meal?"

"Yours was to be sent to your quarters, Sir. And Lady Celeste is dining with Bast in the garden."

"I'll join them."

He made his way there, hearing his concubine's quiet tones and light laughter in response to his first servant's deeper voice long before he found them. A small table had been set up beyond the water feature and dressed with reams of fabric that streamed in the light breeze. Torches were strategically placed to give light without detracting from the gentle ambiance.

The evening had cooled the space to a comfortable level, and Celeste wore a gown similar to the one he'd removed so expeditiously the night before, but in shimmering shades of green. Her hair was still tied high on her head and the nape of her long, slender neck looked vulnerable. He craved to press his lips there and his lower body stirred in agreement.

"Sir." Bast shoved to his feet and stared. Celeste inched around in her chair and gave him a cool smile. If she was surprised, she hid it admirably, and Lysett understood the concern his first servant had voiced earlier. Did he really want this cool, distant female, a mere political partner? He struggled with the answer.

Vorst hurried past with dishes and utensils, a napkin trailing in his wake. He saved Lysett the necessity of explaining why he was there, so he chose a chair and sat to Celeste's right.

"I'll return with additional food." Vorst rushed away and Bast stared after him.

"How nice of you to join us." There wasn't a hint of sarcasm in Celeste's voice or any on her face. She poured him a glass of ale and offered a plate of some form of starters, primarily vegetables. He filled a small dish without comment and wished he had eaten in his quarters after all. *Coward.*

"I was explaining the presentation," Bast said.

"So you're aware all the Houses will attend. As well as a certain number from the public." Lysett tried to look into Celeste's beautiful eyes but was met with a blank wall.

She sipped at her juice and nodded. "As Bast said."

"You and I will present a united front and set the example."

"And what example is that?" Her words reflected simple curiosity and her limpid gaze nothing but interest, but he intuited something else hidden there.

"It's imperative that the dissenters, the purists, not receive any fodder to build their platform on. Unless we determine who they are and their plans, beforehand. Regardless, the populace must be convinced this plan is for the future of Meridia."

"Your emissions over the last months have been effective, Sir." Bast sounded reassuring and positive.

"So I understand, but there is nothing like seeing for oneself."

"Bast has explained how I must comport myself," Celeste offered.

"And how is that?" he asked her.

"With dignity and a certain aloofness, yet with a general appeal. I confess it sounds like a difficult task, but I'll do my best."

"You should be yourself." He spoke brusquely and both Bast and Celeste visibly leaned away from him. "You don't strike me as the aloof type, Celeste, and it will come across as counterfeit. Be yourself."

"I'm not sure what that even means anymore." She spoke so quietly he barely heard her, especially with the burbling water in the background.

"Excuse me?"

She shook her head. "Nothing, Ruler. I won't disappoint you."

"You can count on me to lead you, Celeste. Those attending will be convinced."

She studied him for a long moment, and he tried

to read her, grasping at the flash of naked emotion she so quickly veiled. "I won't disappoint," she repeated, and reached for a bite on her plate, throwing up that wall between them.

He and Bast next spoke of the hunt for the dissenters, in the most general of terms, not wishing to alarm Celeste, though the danger was real. His first servant rose to the occasion as always, and he thought his concubine was deferring to their conversation when she spoke.

"I understand the thought is to kill us and remove any chance of Earth DNA from polluting the Meridian gene pool."

His appetite gone, Lysett turned to her. "That won't happen. It's a small contingent and far too many of our politicos and a number of our warriors have found their chosen ones. Matches have been made and it's highly unlikely the males will allow anything to happen to their concubines."

"The matches have been that successful."

"Indeed, they have. I had no idea Meridia's males could wax so poetic, touting their concubine's attributes. In a respectful manner," he hurriedly added.

In fact, he'd been inundated with positive regard for the process, and Ashtun's happiness was a reflection of many of the matches. The concubines were treasured and above price. As his thoughts warred with his own reticence and reserve toward Celeste, she stood, carefully stepping away from the table.

"Please excuse me. I find I'm tired. I'm not used to working long hours in the garden after such a hiatus, and my visit with Shirley wore me out." She smiled in his general direction and touched a hand to Bast's forearm, a mere graze that made Lysett set his teeth for no reason he could discern.

Both he and his first servant clambered to their feet as she moved gracefully toward the house. Morat fell in behind her and Lysett quelled the instinct to escort her himself.

"I don't care for the idea that she is fearful for her safety. I won't allow anything to happen to her," he told Bast.

"She didn't seek her room because of fear, Master." Bast waited for him to sit before taking his own seat and taking up a fork.

"Then why?" He noted her nearly full plate and glass, making a mental note to have something sent to her quarters. It wouldn't do for her not to eat properly, especially as she could already be breeding.

"I suspect the talk of successful matches contrasted with the political connection you yourself have made with Lady Celeste, and she finds herself lacking. But she has resigned herself and I doubt you'll ever hear her complain." Bast's words were delivered in a quiet, factual manner, but the reproach was detectable.

"You test me, Bast. I would have thought that you, of anyone, would understand that my heart's loyalty is to Lady Trosan. To her memory."

The other male closed his eyes and took a deep breath. Lysett watched the other man's throat work as he swallowed and braced himself for another unpalatable insight. He wondered that he allowed Bast such liberties, but said nothing to dissuade him.

Finally, his first servant said, "I grieve her loss as you do, Ruler. She was the perfect political partner, your astute equal on that front, and a dear friend. Her sacrifice will never be forgotten or go unnoticed. But she would have wanted you to move forward and live your life. And if that includes an arrangement to bring you joy, I'm certain she would have wanted that too."

Bast's heartfelt words washed over him like a salve in the flickering light of the torches and gave him pause. He wondered if he was being fair to Celeste, recalling her wish to refuse him and his response to that desire. Perhaps she would have found another match and the male would have made her happy in it. He didn't think he had it within him to complete that particular task, but he couldn't let her go. Selfish, but for the right reasons. Definitely, the right reasons. He would think on them and collate them in a minute. In any event, it was too late. The joining had taken place—at her request—and she might even now be with child. She was stuck with him. *So why not call in the healer?*

Ignoring the question, he formulated a plan. He'd make an effort to spend more time with her and set aside his ambivalent feelings. It wasn't her fault that Celeste followed in the footsteps of a wonderful female. He hadn't given her the chance to actually live up to her reputation, and show herself outside of their physical compatibility. He would make that effort and perhaps a friendship would develop past the physicality. He'd appreciated and respected her before they even met, and after all, they would be raising children together.

"Thank you for your insight, Bast. And that is the last you are to speak of such things."

"Understood, Sir."

Chapter Ten

"There are too many choices," Celeste protested.

Ellyce smiled widely and tugged yet another gown from the rack. "Try this one. It has a thread running throughout that matches your eyes. You concubines display such variety with your hair and especially eye color. The difference in our pupils aside, it's such a pleasure to see the diversity. There are a few with green eyes, but so many with brown ones and blue. Even some gray and what I understand is … hazel?"

"Hazel. That's right. That eye color changes with mood or with what a person is wearing." She struggled into the gown, and nearly staggered beneath its weight. "This is too heavy. Too encrusted with those shiny layers."

"The shiny layers are precious gems, daughter."

Celeste froze in the act of letting the dress slip off her shoulders to the floor. "Holy cow. Sorry. I—" She didn't know if her reaction was because of the implied value of the garment or because the Ruler's mother had called her *daughter*.

Laughing, Ellyce grasped the garment and handed her another, this one in a warm shade of brown with silver shot through it. "See if you like this one. And don't worry about the cost. Lysett is wealthy, although he doesn't flaunt it. His concubine will dress tastefully and well."

"You called me daughter." She didn't want to think about how the Ruler dressed his concubines.

"Are you offended? I know your own mother is passed, and I thought…"

"Not offended. But I'm only your son's concubine. I'm not… I don't…" She cast about for the right words. "I'm not like Lady Trosan."

Ellyce studied her, her face solemn and eyes thoughtful. "Ah, so he's told you of her. Good. You should know. They were so very close as children and aspired to the same things politically. It was no surprise when they matched, despite the worry and implications for Trosan. Our scientists and then the medicos did their best but it didn't work out."

"I'm sorry."

"You well know what it's like, Celeste, to lose someone. Many someones. Lysett has told us this. Not everything, because that is for you to share. But he is in awe of your personal strength and abilities, your attributes."

So impressed he figured I'd be a good stand in for Trosan, until he actually met me, face to face. Keeping her features from reflecting any of her thoughts, she let Ellyce fasten the brown dress. Brown was probably the best color. Staid and proper, nothing flashy to detract from the seriousness of her role.

Lysett had put in an appearance at breakfast, inquiring as to her health, whether she'd slept well, and chatted desultorily until he headed out to his other office. The one she hadn't seen because she couldn't leave the house. She figured she was well aware of her role.

After his comments last night about so many of the other matches—arrangements—going well, she'd found she couldn't keep up appearances, and fled. Though Lord knew she needed to practice in the face of what she'd be seeing at the presentation event. No one could know how miserable she was because likely no one would be able to grasp it. There would be any number of women who'd have traded places with her in a heartbeat so she really had to make it work. She didn't want anyone's censure—or pity. Although they'd likely pity

Lysett.

Maybe if she let that secret part of her come forth at the presentation, the one that strained toward the surface whenever she thought about him, let alone was in his presence, then others would think they were as special a couple. For sure they'd see an entranced young woman in lust with their Ruler, a silly girl willing to fall at his feet. But she had her pride, so banished the idea before it grew roots, and resolved to find some other way.

"If you wish, you can call me Mother, instead of Lady Ellyce."

The offer sucked the breath out of her and Ellyce took advantage to tighten the gown further. "Uh, that's a really nice thing to say."

"I already feel a closeness to you. We will have many, many years together as a family."

"I like you, too." And she did, despite knowing calling Ellyce 'Mother' wasn't even close to appropriate. Lysett would choke. She wished the woman knew the parameters her son had set on their arrangement, because if she did, these awkward discussions would surely not take place. The thought of all those years together as a family... Pretending...

"Might you be with child?" The older woman looked uncomfortable asking, but her eyes glinted with hope.

"I don't know yet. I hope so." And she did because then she had a year or better to figure out how to get through another physical encounter with that man without losing herself. And have a sweet baby to cuddle and love, maybe love her back.

"Oh, I hope so, too. The thought of Meridia blessed with children makes my heart sing. I've heard musings that other concubines have conceived, despite the short period of time since they arrived. And the joy that permeates Meridia already... One can actually *feel* the ambiance." Ellyce finished tightening the lacings and urged her to face the mirror.

The young woman staring back sported pale cheeks and shining eyes. Celeste knew both were a result of hearing how happy so many of the other concubines and their men were, mocking her own lack of *joy*. Ellyce didn't know she'd shoved a verbal knife into Celeste's gut.

She blinked away the tears and reconsidered her reflection, straining for composure. No staid matron looked back. The rich, warm, earthy color suited her and the fit subtly enhanced her curves, especially the slope of her breasts. When she moved, the silver threads separated ever so slightly and hinted at creamy flesh beneath. One could almost believe she fit the bill.

The other woman winked at her conspiratorially and nodded. "Stunning. We'll leave your hair down for the most part but braid it here … and here, to show off the shape and color of your eyes."

"You don't think it's too much for such an important event?" Maybe she could impress the others by hiding behind the look.

"You'll appear every inch an exotic royal concubine. As different from Trosan as can be imagined, which is Lysett's plan, I believe."

Her belly clenched and she swallowed rusty-tasting saliva, the beauty of the gown and the way it brought out the best in her thoroughly spoiled. He'd said for her to be herself. The woman in the mirror wasn't her. He should make up his mind. She shook her head. "I don't think so. I'd like something plainer. More me."

Obviously flustered, Ellyce drew her brows together. "But you look lovely."

"I don't look like *me*, Lady Ellyce." Her failure to use the more intimate term was noted, and the other woman's face fell. Celeste felt cruel and it made her even more despondent, but she couldn't let herself get sucked in any deeper.

"I've upset you somehow." Ellyce wrung her hands.

Knowing her smile looked phony, she kept it pasted on her lips and impulsively hugged Ellyce, who, after a startled moment, hugged her back. "Everything has been overwhelming and moved so fast. I can't... I can't seem to find my feet, and this event is important. It's all I can focus on right now."

"Of course. I'm a selfish old woman, excited about babies and wanting you to call me a familiar, when this is so overwhelming for you. No, don't protest. We'll find you something more ... you."

****

The garden was fast becoming her sanctuary. The guards were ever present yet never intruded, and Bast was in tune with her moods. She was willing to rebuild their comfortable relationship as much as possible, and in turn, he never mentioned the Ruler, at least not in a personal context. She idly turned a spoon over and over before using it to scoop out a bite of fruit from its skin. She had her suitable gown for the presentation, a plain length of blue fabric sewn in severe, classic lines— nothing to make her stand out, yet conveying a quiet strength of classic elegance, she hoped.

She'd acquiesced to Lysett's mother's insistence that the shade at least match her eyes. Ellyce promised to assist with her hair and bring the jewelry she held in safekeeping for the Ruler's concubine. Celeste didn't want to accept anything to remind him of what—who— he'd lost but Ellyce told her she had an item in mind that had never been worn. Celeste wondered if the older woman was beginning to intuit that all was not so *joyful* on the home front, and cursed her inability to be more convincing. The way she excused herself to return to her own home and not stay for refreshments with Celeste spoke volumes.

"May I join you?" Bast hovered by the table.

"Sure." She'd given up trying to emulate the Meridian's stilted speech patterns, although it served to keep Lysett at a distance because he responded predictably. She'd never have gotten away from the table last night to lick her wounds if she hadn't pled tiredness and whined like a weak-witted girl.

"I haven't time to eat. I'm in between offices, but you looked lost in thought. Are you all right?"

"I'm fine." Maybe she should change that to 'good'. A little variety in her faking it. "A little tired after the mad home shopping spree is all."

"Lady Ellyce is a kind female and is delighted that you are part of the family."

She wasn't part of the family, but he could say so. "She's really nice."

"Do you have any questions about the upcoming presentation?"

"No."

"Are you worried?"

"Worried? About messing it up? For sure. But all I can do is try to act the part. I won't embarrass your master." She'd hide someplace first.

"You couldn't if you tried. He is lucky to have you."

That surprised her, but she didn't let it show, choosing another piece of fruit to cover her reaction. "You've done everything to describe it except draw me a picture, Bast. There will be a banquet and a few speeches—not that I have to say a word, thank goodness—and a bunch of introductions. I can smile and nod and clasp hands—briefly—and perhaps say a few things. But say nothing about their House or what they wear. Maybe comment on the weather. Right?"

"That sums it up, Lady. They are aware of your ability to lead and how you stirred the other females to mutiny on the ship. Such behavior is much admired, possibly because our females were once warriors. And of course, I've let it be known how kind you are, as well as your other attributes. They will, however, expect you to be circumspect and … regal. And they will watch to see if you and our Master … are connected."

Inwardly rolling her eyes, Celeste took stock of her so-called attributes. What use were those here on Meridia, with the exception of her fertility? She had no other particular skills to be put to use. They might wonder why Lysett had chosen her, in that she was no beauty to draw the eye. She shuddered to think anyone other than the three of them knew he hadn't laid eyes on her until the night he'd first thought to … breed her, and the resulting debacle.

"You are thinking dark thoughts."

"No, not dark. Only ones colored with self-pity. I'm sick of myself." It was okay to share that with a friend, right? She was spiraling again, and would find herself stuck if she didn't smarten up.

"It is all right, Lady Celeste. You're overwhelmed, understandably."

Everyone kept saying that. No, she was caught in a trap of her own making and needed to find a way to make the best of it. "I need to get over myself. And I'd like you to call me Celeste when it's just the two of us. Please."

"I'll try." Bast gave her a bracing smile, but his

eyes were clouded with concern.

She waved him to the door and settled in to pick through her meal and rehash how she might comport herself in front of all those other people. Morat shifted his weight, and the rustle of his tunic drew her attention. Celeste looked at his serious face and wished she could strike up a conversation with the guard, but he didn't appear to like her any more than Lysett did, though treated her with the same distant respect.

He stared back impassively for a moment before scanning the area the way he usually did. Something in his face as he did so made her blink. Was that distaste? With an inner shrug, she poured another glass of water. Morat probably wanted to be off doing warrior things instead of babysitting a female, particularly when it was unlikely he'd have a concubine for himself.

Swirling the liquid around in the crystal-like container, Celeste wondered if there would be more Earth women willing to leave their planet and join with Meridian males. Especially if they were confronted with the happy unions being touted. She hoped she didn't have to be an emissary because she couldn't think of a less convincing one.

With a sigh, she set her lips in a faint smile— there was no time like the present to practice looking aloof yet happy—and pushed up from the table.

"I hoped I'd be back in time to share the meal with you."

Shocked, she sat back down with an inelegant slump, and swallowed her heart into its proper position in her chest. Lysett regarded her from only a few feet away.

"I'm finished, actually."

"Perhaps you'll take … tea, while I eat."

Nodding, she waited as he ordered the beverage and added his own food requests. Surreptitiously, she scanned his tall, lithe frame, and quelled the frisson sparking in her belly. She supposed it was a positive thing that her body desired him and only wished she might keep the rest of her separate. A one-sided emotional connection would spell heartbreak.

When her gaze settled on his face, she noted the tiredness around his remarkable green eyes. Impulsively, she spoke. "You look as though it was a difficult day."

Instantly, he met her stare while settling into the chair opposite. He obviously chose his words, and her heart sank further. What did they have in common, really? What did she have to offer him when he came home looking thus? Her mother would have embraced her husband and said soft things for his ears only, and coaxed the source of his angst from him. Celeste was dealt another crippling blow as she accepted she'd truly longed for such a union, despite the pain that would inevitably accompany any of the loss. She hurt now, and without the kind of connection her parents had shared to buffer it.

Lysett was speaking, and she strove to give him her attention. "Merely the usual issues of governing, Celeste. You won't be familiar with them. But it's nothing new to me, and to be expected."

"Of course," she murmured. "I'm sorry there's nothing I can do."

"Do?" He eyed her with something etching his features she hesitated to decipher. "You will fulfill your role, my concubine. I have no doubt of that. What more could I ask of you?"

Right. Indeed. She had that assigned role and would focus on it. Ignoring the welter of emotions she'd resolved to deal with earlier, Celeste nodded again and was grateful when Vorst approached with her tea and Lysett's dishes. She pretended to sip at her cup, counting the minutes when she could believably request her dismissal.

"What do you miss most?"

Nearly choking on the fragrant brew, she blinked and made herself look at the handsome man sitting so close she could scent him. "Miss?"

"From Earth."

"My friend, I suppose." She didn't miss the drafty old house with its sketchy garden and her miserly possessions. Meridia—the Ruler—had promised to provide for her and so he had. She should be grateful.

"Who is this friend?" His tone had a sharp edge to it.

"Laurel, my neighbor. She and her husband were the only people I felt I could trust."

"Ah, a female. And she wasn't among those … escorted here?" Lysett seemed to relax and applied himself to his meal.

"Laurel is past childbearing age," she replied dryly.

He didn't reply and didn't look at her either. Celeste couldn't help but feel a hint of satisfaction in reminding him how selective his troops had been. "I hope I might get word back to her at some point."

His stare returned to hers. "That might be possible."

A gust of air escaped her lungs. "Really?"

"Once we are certain the resistance to Earth concubines has been dealt with, there is the hope we might *negotiate* additional females being placed with our males. It would empower our cause if you were seen as happily placed here, and that would require a visit to Earth."

Celeste resisted the urge to scan the room for mind reading paraphernalia. Hadn't she just been thinking similar thoughts? She bit her tongue against protesting her suitability to be held up as a shining example. Lysett must be deluding himself, and his mother and his first servant were perpetuating the myth, but one thing at a time. The idea of seeing Laurel again twisted her belly with homesickness. With an effort, she kept her response calm and cool. "I'd love to see my friend."

"You can't travel while you are breeding, but we'll coordinate such a trip in the future."

It all came down to his requirements. Certain she'd scream if she had to listen to another word, she set her tea down. "I'd like to go to bed. I'm tired."

Was it her imagination, or did those green eyes flare, the pupils dilate? "Of course. I regret the lateness of the hour once again." He stood and offered his hand.

Willing herself not to feel anything from his touch, she set her fingers on top of his, and levered to her feet, then quickly pulled her hand away. The warmth lingered nonetheless and she nervously clutched the stuff of her dress. "Good night."

"I'll escort you."

Wondering if he knew she was fleeing, despite her attempt to slow her footsteps, Celeste gained the stairs and hurried up them, aware of the heated bulk of the Ruler right behind her. She forced herself to measure the distance to her door and reached for the knob, only to be forestalled by Lysett's big hand wrapping around her own. She shivered.

"Are you cold?"

"No. I'm tired. Good night."

"Celeste." He set his hands on her shoulders and gently turned her to face him, drawing her close. "There *is* something you might do for me."

Setting her lips against a tremor, she swallowed

and made herself look up at him. "And what is that?"

The glide of fingertips down the length of her spine stole her breath, and when he cupped a buttock in his palm, she nearly cried out. He bent and set his mouth on hers, absorbing any other sound she might have made, and traced the seam of her lips with his tongue. Almost involuntarily, she parted them to allow him entrance, vaguely aware he had fit her tightly against him. She felt the hard planes of his chest connect with her swelling breasts—and the bold thrust of his cock against her center.

"I would have you again, tonight," he murmured beside her cheek.

Her voice of self-preservation clamored against the din created by his proximity, and the magic his touch was weaving. She struggled to find the words to disengage and came up empty, managing only a frail shake of her head.

"Celeste? Don't deny me. I seek your comfort."

Wasn't that what she wanted to offer? Was it enough? It was too little for her, but sometimes half a loaf... Knowing she'd regret it, yet powerless to refuse, she bowed her head in surrender.

Lysett gathered her into his arms and strode away down the hall, shoving past a startled Morat. Celeste squeezed her eyes shut in embarrassment and breathed in the Ruler's familiar smell. She'd know him anywhere, for the rest of her life, his scent filed away to be stored with both happy and painful reminders. Nestled against the hard planes of his chest, she wondered where he was taking her.

Moments later, a door hissed open and she chanced a look through lowered lids. A spacious room filled her vision and a high, very large bed, dressed in dark gold and green fabrics drew her attention. They were in his apartments. A tiny part of her wondered if this was significant before he lowered her to the mattress, the intent look on his face giving it a near-feral appearance. She wasn't fearful. The emotion he telegraphed caused her own need to unfurl. She felt it etch its symptoms upon her own features, her eyes widening, skin flushing and her breath deepening as her lips parted to gasp in more air. As if it was a signal, Lysett pounced.

He stripped her gown away with brisk, efficient movements, pausing only to coast his fingertips over her thrusting nipples before dealing with her undergarments. Her shiver and resulting arch into his hands elicited a dark smile before he tore at his own clothes. She got a glimpse of all that muscled, golden flesh on display before he was on her again.

Caged by his bulk, sweetly crushed, she reveled in the sensation of his skin on hers. Soft and smooth flesh slid against slightly hair-roughened and created a delightful dichotomy as he rubbed over her, the thickness of his sex prodding damply at her belly.

"I—" He set his mouth as she stared up into his face, willing her own passivity when she desperately wanted to put her hands on him. His head shook faintly and his lids lowered as if he was searching for the right thing to say.

Taking a risk, she turned her head to his shoulder and pressed a kiss there. His eyes flew open and she drowned in the wealth of emotion displayed. Before she could hope to decipher them, he took her mouth, and with it, her ability to think.

His big hands grasped her waist, then slipped beneath her, drawing her even closer as if to imprint himself. In a sudden move, he flipped their bodies and she found herself sprawled on an intensely provocative mattress with intriguing dips and … protrusions. Rough palms slid over her back to cup her buttocks before traversing her upper thighs.

Embarrassingly wet, she squirmed and her folds teased his shaft. Lysett tore his lips from hers and she thought she heard him … growl? The rumbling sound denoted barely leashed passion as she marked the tension of his big body, and wished to soothe him.

"Are you able to take me, Celeste?"

Could she? Her core ached for release, for him. She nodded, and he lifted his hips to grind himself against her.

"Put me inside."

Spreading her legs, she set a knee on either side of his hips, fully aware of his avid stare as it raked her body. One hand came up to flirt with a nipple and distracted her from her task. Lysett chuckled when she threw him a disgruntled look. This hardly seemed passive, and her hand shook as she tentatively grasped his cock.

Softness over steel filled her fingers and she closed them around him as far as she could. His muted groan startled her and she instantly released her hold.

"No. Don't stop." He gave her what was likely meant to be a reassuring smile, but looked more desperate than anything else. "Continue."

With more confidence, she clasped him again, taking the opportunity to stroke his length and drift her fingertips over the wide head. He groaned again, this time loudly, and she wished she might continue her exploration, especially downward to the firm sac she knew held his testicles.

Afraid of overstepping, she turned her attention to placing herself in a position to facilitate putting him inside, raising her body up and shifting forward. Her thighs quivered.

"You may touch me, Celeste. As I touched you." He regarded her from between languidly lowered lids.

Such a thing would definitely not be passive, and she hesitated, thinking of how he had touched—explored—her. Encouraged by his nod, she stroked him from root to tip and cupped his heavy sac in her other hand. Lysett hardened further, flexing beneath her fingers as she continued her ministrations.

Moistening her lips, she ventured a kiss on the silky skin, inhaling his musky heat. He muttered under his breath and heaved a great breath when she kissed and licked along the shaft of his penis, then sucked the head into her mouth.

"By the Goddess, Celeste," he groaned. He wove his fingers through her hair and directed her movements.

Emboldened, she used her tongue to mimic his actions from when he pleasured her and intermittently sucked, losing herself in pleasing him, until he tugged her head upward.

"Did I do it wrong?" She touched her mouth, finding her lips wet and swollen.

"Not wrong, Celeste, but I wish to spend inside of you."

His words crashed over her like a spill of cold water. Procreation. This was about making a child. She froze and tried not to think about anything other than that. Pleasure was secondary—and anything else.

"Celeste." His tone was gentle, and he smoothed her hair away from her face, tugging the tendrils over her shoulders. He cupped her breasts and leaned up to suckle, first one, then the other, creating splintering shards of awareness that manifested in her groin as his belly rippled against her thighs.

Taking her hand, he placed it on his cock and

urged her to raise up, his other hand smoothing over her hip. Unfamiliar, she centered her body over their hands and he positioned his cock at her entrance. "Take your time. Go at your own pace."

The head of his shaft slipped inside, eased by her natural lubricant as she cautiously lowered herself. Lysett drew their hands away and grasped her hips, supporting her. Inch by inch she took him deeper, filling her up until his sac brushed her buttocks.

On display and intimately impaled, her cheeks heated until she let herself meet his stare. That feral look was back, yet she sensed it was her who was in charge and wondered if he'd allowed it or it was because of the circumstance.

"Can you move? Ride me?" His questions emerged from between gritted teeth and she suspected he was barely holding on.

She wasn't sure if riding him meant what he inferred, but she began to lift and lower herself on his shaft, experimenting with the depth. At first, she was able to focus on leaning forward and then back to increase the friction and found a rhythm that built delicious sensation. Once again losing herself, she strained toward release when Lysett sought out her apex and worked the knot of nerves with his thumb.

His forehead and upper lip glistened with sweat and his jaw clenched. Celeste sped up her movements, now choppy and frantic, and shuddered into a climax when Lysett drove upward to meet her. His face twisted in serene agony before he drew her onto his heaving chest, where she lay, dissolved.

Boneless and replete, she didn't resist when he eased her onto the bed and tugged a covering over her.

"I'll be back shortly."

Chapter Eleven

The morning brought unanswerable questions for Lysett. Why had he brought her here? To his quarters? He hadn't cared to breach her own space last night, understanding she required some privacy, but there were other places. Even the one with the breeding pallet...

His royal concubine slept, huddled in on herself beneath the bed linens, and he had no idea how he was going to return her to her own rooms without appearing callous. And did he even want to do so? He had hurt her so many times already, according to Bast—and his own conscience. A certain part of his anatomy twitched, suggesting Celeste remain exactly where she was for the foreseeable future, and Lysett tamped down his animal lust, unsuccessfully.

Gone was his determination to keep her at arm's length and maintain a political marriage—he couldn't stop thinking about her naked in his arms, and losing himself in her sweet body. Even now, though surely he should be replete after the number of times he'd woken her in the night to position her small form in every way imaginable... And how she'd received him without complaint, indeed with such passion that he had indeed lost himself in her. Clenching his fists, he made himself turn away.

He knew she was unhappy, her sadness simmering beneath the surface of composure, now he allowed himself to see it. And he acknowledged that perhaps he was the primary cause, having listened to Bast more keenly that his first servant was aware. Hence his effort to spend more time with her, regardless of the excuse he'd tried to give himself. Was he making things worse? She'd said she accepted their joining to beget an heir and maintained that distance herself. Last night—much of the night—hadn't been about mere joining. He had craved her with such reckless need that he hardly knew himself and her pleasure had surely eased her sorrow.

Raking a hand through his hair, he considered the intimacy of what they'd shared. She had comforted him with her body, but he wanted more. He wanted the female Bast had described, without the burden he'd placed on her because of his grief. Lysett of the House of Daboort was known as a fair ruler, and the last thing he'd been to Celeste was fair.

She slept quietly, immune to his heavy thoughts, and he strode to the bathing room to cleanse and prepare for the day. He still couldn't label this … thing between them and wasn't certain she felt it as well but knew he had to work it out. He and his concubine needed to converse, and soon.

Emerging from his ablutions, wearing only a towel slung around his hips, he staggered to a sudden halt. His bed was empty, his gaze drawn there immediately. Only a jumble of covers suggested his concubine had recently slumbered there. He cursed under his breath. He should have woken her, cleansed with her… The thought of her small frame deluged with a stream of water while he drew the lather over her curves and her small hands caressed his own body— Lysett wrenched his carnal thoughts in a different direction.

Who knew what his concubine had thought when she roused and found herself alone? Did she regret the night in his bed? Was she fleeing from him and rebuilding her own walls? He frowned. How had she left his quarters? They needed to talk, now.

Snatching up a robe, he shouldered into the clinging fabric and settled it around his frame with another curse. Throwing open the door, he stalked the length of the corridors until he reached her room. As he rapped firmly, he was cast back in time to this very same behavior of that unfortunate night. Perhaps he'd never learn. When there was no response, he knocked harder and again received no reply. It vaguely registered that her guard was nowhere in sight, and his senses pricked.

"Celeste!" Was she ignoring him, or perhaps in her own bathing room? "Celeste!"

Pressing his palm against the sensor, he willed the panel to slide open more quickly. A yawning emptiness greeted him, and he quickly moved throughout the space. With no sign of her, he surmised she had gone downstairs to eat, or perhaps to the garden. But neither sat well. As disheveled as she was, Celeste would, at the very least, have changed and showered. He shoved away a sickening fear and called for a guard.

"Ruler." A large individual instantly presented himself. "I am Vikte."

"Where is Lady Celeste?"

The other male squinted. "Sir? I believed her to be with you."

"Where is her personal guard?"

"Morat? He…" Vikte's brow creased. "He has left. The primary saw him leaving with his belongings. Even those from his locker. I was assigned here. I assumed he was taking leave."

A vast chill descended over him. While it froze his heart, his brain focused and sifted through Morat's personal information. "Take She-at and attend Morat's family home." He rattled off the directions, though knew it was too simple. Morat would never go to ground with Celeste in such a familiar location. The thought of her small body bound and confined within the traitor's travel duffle— "Go quickly!"

The guard moved swiftly, calling out for She-at, and Lysett turned on his heel to rush back to his quarters to dress, summoning Bast on the run. His first servant arrived, out of breath and clothing awry.

"Morat? How is this possible, Master? I assigned him myself and he welcomed the honor of guarding the royal concubine. There was no sign he was part of the resistance. He—"

"The purists don't advertise, Bast. Get Ashtun here with troops we believe to be loyal. We have the inhabitants of a smaller House to interrogate." He wasn't going to think the worst. They wouldn't want a martyr, so would likely be planning to make an example of his concubine. He nearly doubled over when he thought of the ways that might be achieved. Better she die than face the latter.

****

This was definitely not the Ruler's quarters. Waking up in Lysett's big bed earlier had been a surreal experience. Initially, she'd had no idea where she was, stretching languidly before the enormity of her situation burst upon her. A cautious peek ascertained she was alone, and she'd then taken note of the information her body was sharing. Her breasts were tender, the nipples chafed, and a blush washed up to color her cheeks as she remembered the feel of his mouth on her there. Usually clean shaven, the Ruler had sported faint stubble—and she recalled the sensation against other delicate skin, her blush intensifying.

The memory of her first night with him was something she'd wrapped up and stored away, only to take out and examine when she thought she might cope—and that had been never. There was no way she would be able to lock up the memories now. He'd engaged her full participation in unleashing this … this sexual need. It bordered on voraciousness because he didn't even have to be in the room for her belly to clench with need and her sex to soften and swell. The mere thought...

She needed a bath. Not that Lysett hadn't cleansed his seed from her following the myriad of times he'd— No, she couldn't place the blame on his shoulders, at least not all of it. *They* had indulged in such pleasurable acts. She'd been a very willing participant, and if she wasn't so embarrassed, she might take a curious pride in knowing little, inexperienced Celeste Raynor had made the Ruler groan with gratification. And he'd said things to her, albeit in his own language, but she understood enough Meridian to know they were tender things, maybe even loving things?

But it was the morning after, and no doubt he would go back to acting all aloof and royal as if *this* hadn't happened at all. Until the next time... It was as though she were two people, and she somehow had to follow his example and keep them separate. Somehow. Her chest constricted and she struggled for air. There was no manual for her to follow insofar as her response went, not when it came to this. She couldn't face him, at least not until she could rebuild the wall he'd effortlessly torn down.

Clambering to the edge of the bed, she had slipped to the floor, her toes curling against the cool tiles. Her dress lay strewn over a chair, and she hunted for her underthings. Finding only her panties, she struggled into them, her hands hesitating as her sex throbbed with delicious soreness. Had he put a child in her? After a tentative touch to her belly, she tugged her dress over her head and smoothed it down. Her breasts sat loosely against the fabric, but there was no help for it. Her room wasn't far, and if she hunched a little and ducked her head, surely her guard wouldn't notice.

He won't be surprised. He knows you were in the Ruler's bed. Save her from her own thoughts. She'd fought another blush and hurried to the door, then heard the sound of water running in the bathing room. Unable to face Lysett before she could raise her shields, she had set her palm against the sensor, praying the system would recognize her. Nothing. She'd tried again, and stepped back in frustration—and the panel had grudgingly slid open to reveal Morat.

Her guard looked as surprised as she felt. His usually stoic face softened dramatically, and his eyes popped. She had thought it puzzling that he was able to access Lysett's quarters but dismissed the vagrant thought as she managed her discomfiture.

"Lady Celeste." Morat shifted awkwardly.

"Is there a problem? The Ruler is cleansing."

Straightening, he'd adopted his usual demeanor. "Bast sent me. You are to be escorted to a safe place."

"What?" She resisted his grip on her arm as he drew her into the hall and the panel shut behind her. "What's happened?"

He had glared over her shoulder at the door, and she found it strange. "Bast will explain. He is on his way to converse with the Ruler. You are to come with me."

"I need to cleanse and change."

"There is no time, Lady." His hold tightened and she had winced, studying his face. It hadn't felt right.

"I want to speak with your master first, Morat."

Something flashed in his other hand and he pressed it against her neck in a lightning move. A sharp, painful twinge had overpowered her senses and her body refused to obey her. The floor rushed up, but Morat dragged her roughly over his shoulder as everything faded out.

And now, waking for the second time, she was aware of his duplicity. He'd hidden his xenophobia fairly well, although perhaps this was about something else. She knew kidnappers wanted something in for returning their victims. Perhaps Lysett would see a value in ransoming her…

Celeste quit her maudlin whining. She had herself to depend on and began to explore her surroundings. As a prison cell went, it was clean, if Spartan, and boasted a narrow bed with a thin coverlet. There was a small adjoining room, and it held a toilet and sink. The only door out was locked, of course, and the window covered with some sort of impervious material. She tried to shift it, and while it seemed thin, there was no give. There was nothing she could fashion into a weapon either. So she had only her wits.

Taking a seat on the bed, she stilled her racing thoughts and refused to think about her present situation. It did no good to reminisce about last night either, so she immersed herself in happier memories of her family and succeeded in achieving a calmer state of mind.

She had no idea how much time elapsed before the door slid open and a male Meridian sauntered into the room. His flashy clothing and swagger didn't compensate for his sloped shoulders or smaller stature. She'd thought all males on Meridia were cut from the same cloth, large and well made, but this man was a pale imitation. Not that she was comparing him to Lysett.

"Ah, the Earth female chosen as the royal concubine." His sneer didn't improve his appearance, and his glance swept over her as if she was nothing. She didn't respond.

"You will rise in my presence. Or kneel."

Considering the way his fist clenched, Celeste got to her feet. She didn't have to look up at him, at least not any distance, and despite the situation, barely quashed a giggle. He preened like the bantam rooster who pretended to rule her yard, back when she had chickens. Her thoughts sobered quickly. Roosters weren't known for their smarts. They had no appreciation of their size and sparred with anything they perceived to be a threat to their little kingdom. But she wasn't kneeling for him.

"Your name."

Surely he knew who she was? "Celeste Raynor."

"I am Quentan of the House of Yehudda." He said it as though she should recognize the name.

"I wish I could say it was nice to meet you."

His eyes narrowed and he glared. "This is not a social occasion, Celeste Raynor. You are a whore and beneath my notice. You will serve one purpose only."

"Excuse me?"

"I am aware of what humans who sell their bodies are called. My cousin infiltrated the envoys to your planet early on, and understands your culture. He supported your males in discouraging human females from even considering Lysett's offer, but there were many of those females, such as yourself, who grasped the opportunity to avail themselves of our planet's riches. By offering your bodies as trade."

A *whore*? Maybe a concubine was just a glorified one? "I'm a concubine, like your female Meridians."

A glancing blow spun her to crash upon the bed, and she scrambled to put some distance between her and this Quentan. Her cheek stung and her eyes watered. He advanced, glowering, and there was nothing but a narrow green ring surrounding his dilated pupils. He looked … crazy.

"Earth females are not concubines," he shouted, spittle coating his thin lips. "The House of Daboort would pollute our bloodlines and contaminate our planet with mongrels. I won't have it. My followers won't have it!"

Making herself as small as possible, she regarded him warily, looking toward the open door, wondering if she could get past him… She risked making him angrier. "Why am I here?"

Quentan visibly regained control, wiping at his mouth and smoothing his ruffled tunic over his bony chest. His breathing returned to normal and his eyes showed only that elongated slice of black in the middle of the pale green. He looked down his nose at her and huffed. "I had hoped that Morat would find the *Ruler*"— he nearly spat the title at her—"abed, an easy target while he rutted upon you. That first servant, Bast, could never have covered up the slaughter of the Ruler *and* his concubine, and my goal would have been reached. But Morat was incompetent and wasted his chance. He could only gain access to the Ruler's quarters the one time and the fool claims you foiled him."

Had she? When she'd left Lysett's room, Morat had been right outside. *Had* her presence kept him from entering? The door had slid closed behind her… A bubble of relief enclosed her heart and pushed away the fear. Lysett was safe.

"What? Nothing to say? You hardly look the warrior type." Quentan's stare raked over her again. "But you sacrificed yourself for the precious Ruler, so you'll be the one to deliver my message. In addition, Lysett might not survive the loss of yet another concubine, regardless of your pathetic worth, and thus, I shall prevail."

She didn't need to ask about his message. He appeared to be the head of the purist movement and lucky her, she was his houseguest. It was like the Searchers all over again, and if she'd felt powerless before…

Quentan paced, waving his hands as he disparaged human females and those Meridians who supported a connection with them. He obviously wasn't looking for a response, carrying on with barely a breath in between imprecations. "Better we become extinct than sully our lines with the likes of you," he finally hissed.

Stepping closer, he wrinkled his face. "You bear his marks and his scent. I am disgusted."

Celeste covered the base of her throat with one hand, sadly noting the absence of her mother's necklace before remembering how Lysett had suckled her there. She knew she smelled like him, knew their joining had imprinted upon her, and she desperately wanted to live and see him again.

Her kidnapper loomed over her, and she felt the evil emanating from his body. His hand shot out and grasped her hair, dragging her toward him. She made him work for it, making her body slack and heavy, even as her scalp burned and strands of her hair tore free, then pushed off hard with both feet. The momentum carried them both to the floor, and she scrambled along his body in an effort to gain the door. Two males, both dressed in what she knew to be warrior garb, filled the opening and blocked her attempt. Behind her, Quentan shoved to his feet.

Knowing she'd embarrassed him in front of his guards, she braced for another blow, and he obliged, his face purple with fury. Rolling with it, she escaped most of the impact, though her face now ached on both sides, and her eye began to swell.

Quentan gestured to his guards. "She is to be prepared and brought to me within the hour."

He shoved past the larger males, who studied her curiously. Celeste shifted her body and slipped the dagger she'd purloined from Quentan's belt between the folds of the coverlet. The guards were clearly interested in her, regardless if they supported their master in his antipathy. If they attacked, she was going to use that ridiculous weapon, all encrusted in precious stones and obviously a sop to Mr. Bantam Rooster's delusion of grandeur. She might not be able to deter them but was willing to die trying. What awaited her would be far worse, she knew it. The Rooster was nuts.

But the guards moved back into the hall and a stooped, older female entered the room. She had a swath of fabric tossed over her shoulder, and a basket trailed from one arm. She didn't look friendly, not like Ellyce, and her words didn't change Celeste's opinion.

"Whore. Attend me." The old woman plodded into the adjoining room. One of the guards, a stalwart fellow with a glint in his eye motioned to Celeste. It was clear that he'd "help" if she didn't acquiesce.

Moving slowly, she slid across the bed, surreptitiously fitting the dagger into the sleeve of her gown, never taking her stare off of the guard. He watched impassively as she made her way to where the other woman waited.

"Remove that. Or the guards will do it for you." The crone pointed at her gown, and Celeste slipped out of the garment, struggling to retain the dagger in its folds.

"And those." Her underwear followed and she stood, uncertainly, holding the wad of fabric.

"Cleanse yourself. Quickly. My son awaits."

She saw the resemblance now. Crazy Quentan had a mother who was obviously complicit in his plans. She complied, stepping into the warm stream of water, setting her clothes on the shelf where they quickly became soaked. The woman made no comment, shaking out the material from her shoulder.

It was a shapeless sack dress of some kind, fabricated from a heavy white cloth, almost like a … shroud. Celeste's mouth dried out and she could barely will herself to wash with the harsh soap that stung her abraded cheeks. Did the Meridians bury their dead in such things? Her imminent demise became tangible and she glanced at the wad of clothing concealing the dagger.

"Hurry." Mrs. Yehudda, or whatever she went by, tapped her foot and sneered. Quentan must have patterned the look after his mother, and Celeste nearly laughed before reining herself in. Hysteria wasn't going to help her. She rinsed her hair and accepted the towel thrust at her, casually sweeping her sodden dress down to her feet where it landed with a dull thud.

The woman didn't appear to notice, merely passed over a brush. "Make yourself presentable. Your destiny awaits."

"My destiny?"

The old female started, as though she didn't expect Celeste to be able to speak. What had Quentan told her about Earth women? What did she know? She wished there was time to try to engage with his mother, perhaps convince her that Celeste and the other women were sentient beings.

"You and those like you cannot defile the bloodlines of Meridia. My son has foretold it. He will execute you for all to see, and others will follow his lead. There will be no Earth concubines here. No other species to join with ours. We will embrace our fate, unsullied." The blank look in her eyes and the rote speech said it all. There wasn't any possibility of getting Mrs. Yehudda to change sides. She wondered where Quentan's father was.

Celeste shuddered as the swathe of white fabric enveloped her, making her formless and a nonentity. She dipped downward to scrabble for the dagger, managing to grasp the hilt and lay the blade along her forearm. It was awkward but with her arms free beneath the shroud, she could fold them against her chest.

"What are you doing?"

"I thought there were shoes?"

"No footwear. Be grateful you are allowed clothing of any sort. My son would have made an example of you naked, but I wouldn't allow him—or any of the true believers—to see you that way." She fingered the shroud. "Your blood will mark the white most effectively. All will receive our message."

The old woman was crazier than her son. She'd probably put him up to this, or at least encouraged him. Celeste clutched her weapon harder and wondered what she should do when a clamor filtered into the room. She heard it first, the other woman then tilting her head and obviously straining to listen. Shouts and screams indicated an altercation.

Without stopping to consider her actions, Celeste pushed the old woman away. Though hardly a shove, the woman stumbled backward, one arm coming up to flail uselessly as her feet came out from under her. She went down in a welter of limbs, her head meeting the edge of the sink with a resounding crack. Celeste winced, and crouched to touch her slack face, but the increasing noises turned her attention to the other room, and survival beckoned. Angling the dagger to slash against the material of the shroud, a gap opened up and she cut one for her other arm and shoved them through.

She stepped forward, but the sack billowed around her, impeding her progress, so she kneeled to slash off a strip of the hem, winding it around her waist in her next movement. Her heart pounded and air sawed in and out of her lungs. She moved quietly, peering through her undamaged eye around the frame, and saw no evidence of the guards. The sounds of battle grew ever closer and she hustled, tentative, but hoping to take advantage of the confusion and somehow make an escape.

Quentan staggered in, his fancy clothes disheveled and marked with blood spatter. He stumbled to a stop when he spotted her and snarled. She'd seen a sick dog look like that once, desperate and wanting to take down anyone in its path and share its misery. Steeling herself, she held the dagger in front of her and focused on his face, hoping he'd telegraph his next move.

"Where is she? What have you done with my mother?" Well, at least he had a heart and some care for his parent.

"In there. She … she's resting."

"What have you done to her?"

"She fell down. She's okay." Celeste hoped she'd be okay, but couldn't find it within herself to worry at that moment.

"Whore."

It was getting old, being dubbed a whore. Belinda had said they were prostituting themselves, but Shirley loved her male, and so did Celeste, not that she'd admit it to anyone, not even herself. Sure, they'd agreed to come here, albeit with encouragement, and the promise of a future but they were giving back. Besides, women had a right to survive, no matter how they did it.

"You're nuts."

"What do you mean by that?" The translator wasn't converting slang, but Quentan must have gotten the gist because he snarled again and reached for the silver weapon on his belt.

She stood no chance against it, having brought a knife to a gun fight, but there was no place to run or hide.

In desperation, she threw herself forward and slashed at him, much the same way as she'd hacked down the insidious vine choking out the old oak tree at home. She connected with his shoulder and upper arm, a gash opening up to flood his tunic with blood, and she danced backward to look for another opening. Her belly clenched with nausea and desperation.

Perhaps because of the close quarters, he struck out with the weapon, its barrel catching her in the temple, and she saw stars as her vision blurred. The dagger slipped from her grasp. She tried to remain upright but sank toward the floor, Quentan bringing the weapon to bear.

A crack of sound filled the air as she collapsed in an ignominious heap, then was buried beneath Quentan's slack form. Curiously, there was no further pain.

"Celeste!" With the familiar voice, Quentan's body rolled away, and warm breath washed across her sore face. "Celeste! She's hurt. Bring a medico!"

Lysett's worried tone skittered across her consciousness and she tried to hang on, willing her eyes to open so she could see him. A cool hand touched her brow, something pressed against her neck, and then she drifted away.

Chapter Twelve

"She will be fine, son. Our best healer has said so. Her injuries have been treated and she will soon wake." His mother patted his hand and smiled. "You must clean up and change your clothes. You won't want Celeste to see you looking as you do."

Lysett scanned himself. He sported a few injuries of his own, obtained in the struggle against those supporting the House of Yehudda. Liaison Ashtun believed the purists to be contained either within that House or one other, and simultaneous raids had been carried out. Amends would be required for the House of Jabari, whose inhabitants were taken aback when his men stormed their compound. While it was true there were no Earth concubines on the premises, it wasn't for a lack of interest. The head of Jabari would be offered the first choice of the next group of Earth females.

He winced. When he thought about it that way, it reeked of dominion and prestige. He would offer the head male the opportunity to *court* an Earth female should one concede. Celeste would approve of that approach. If she woke up. Of course, she was going to wake up.

Nodding to his parent, he rushed to his quarters to cleanse and re-dress. He wanted to be there when his concubine opened her remarkable eyes again, to be the first one she would see. The sight of her falling at the feet of the traitor, her white apparel vividly stained with crimson, and Quentan bringing a weapon to bear, would haunt him for the rest of his days. Another instant and he would have been too late.

Quentan was dead, phased, and his mother under healer care with little hope for survival, her brain synopses irretrievable. Lysett felt nothing but satisfaction in that regard. The fewer fanatics he had to deal with, the better, and it appeared that without those two, the remainder of their House was no longer inspired. In fact, the resistance had been half-hearted once the perimeter had been breached by a helpful person within. Only a few members were as committed and most had died with the first volley.

One male was willing to speak and identified a relative of Quentan's remaining on Earth and presumably continuing to sew the same seeds of fear and discontent. But not for long. Remove the male, and weed out his co-conspirators, if any, and perhaps some reparation and negotiations might take place. As for his own, more personal revenge, he had Morat.

Toweling off, he pulled on clean clothing and spared a glance in the mirror. He continued to appear wild-eyed, out of control, not the calm, purposeful leader most knew. Adrenaline still pumped through his body, and he grimly decided he'd unleash it on the traitorous guard. Bast indicated Morat had resented his status and inability to be considered for a concubine and had settled for a vast sum of wealth, offered by Quentan and his mother.

But first, he would see to his concubine. If he'd lost her... But he hadn't. She would wake and they would have a conversation, one to discuss their relationship and come to a meeting of minds. He would tell her... Lysett swallowed, and wondered if the battle ahead would be far more dangerous than the one he'd just fought to save his concubine. He should return to the status quo and avoid such horrid indecisiveness and become settled within himself. *Coward.*

"She awakes, Ruler." The healer, the one who'd shared the grim news about Trosan, motioned toward

Celeste who lay dead center in her bed, a small figure draped in a light sheet.

He fought a shudder, the fabric as white as that which she'd been wrapped in when he'd stopped Quentan. Lysett had recognized the significance of that sacrificial shroud and he'd ordered it burned, but not before the sight had churned his guts.

Her face now bore only very faint signs of abuse, and he knew they would fade shortly. The mark he'd placed on her in the throes of passion was no longer evident and he supposed the healer had addressed that as well. He hated the thought that the outward evidence of their connection was so easily erased. Kneeling beside the bed, he carefully grasped her hand. "Celeste."

Her long lashes fluttered and lifted, impossibly blue eyes clearing as she met his stare. She looked a question and he guessed. "You are home, and safe. Quentan is dead, his parent incapacitated."

"Is she… I mean…" Her hand familiarly sought her necklace, and he was relieved that he'd placed it about her neck as soon as he'd brought her home.

"You protected yourself as you should, Celeste. She'd have spared no thought for you. There is no need for guilt."

"She cared about her son, and he cared about her."

With a sigh, he nodded. His concubine was indeed blessed with a kind heart. "The head of the House, Quentan's father, Baruk, passed several years ago. His concubine, Jamille, was dealt a harsh blow and evidently became twisted in her thinking."

"Her heart was broken and she went mad."

He studied her, wondering at her understanding. "I suppose that is true. And she lavished all attention on her son, who became less than what one might expect of a warrior, or a politico, for that matter."

"Was it you who stopped Quentan?"

"It was. Though I'd have been happy for anyone to have done so."

She sighed. "Thank you."

Was she thanking him? Thanking the male who had allowed a traitor to guard her and take her from the royal House? To a place where she very nearly died? Lysett stitched on a smile. "There is no need to thank me, Celeste. You fended well for yourself." Despite the emptiness resulting from a resurgence of his terror, he felt a prick of pride for her. A warrior, no matter the circumstances, yet one who submitted to him.

The enormity of what he'd burdened her with sapped his strength, and he bowed beneath the weight of it.

"What's wrong? Were you hurt?" She struggled to sit up, and he hastened to aid her.

"No. I'm fine." He'd heal the few minor injuries on his own, eschewing the healer's help. He needed the reminder of his ineptness … and other things he failed at.

"I'd like something to drink. Tea? Please?"

Bast and his mother vied for entry, each bearing a tray. His father hovered in the doorway, his face turned in Lysett's direction. His guilt and shame were so great he avoided his parent's stare, applying his efforts to ensuring his concubine was comfortable. She sipped at the beverage and managed a few bites before asking him about Morat.

"Morat kidnapped you and transported you to the House of Yehudda. He must have drugged you. The small pocket of purists was ensconced there."

"I know that. But why? Was he a purist, too?"

"No." He explained what he understood of Morat's reasoning. "And I plan to deal with him shortly.

I will make an example of him."

Celeste shook her head. "I might not feel as charitable had he succeeded, Ruler, but wouldn't it be more effective if he made amends?"

He wanted her to call him Lysett, to hear his name pass her sweet lips, and dispense with the formality, the way she'd moaned it in his bed. "That isn't our way, Celeste."

"But you're moving in different ways, Sir. You've brought Earth females here to ensure the survival of your species. Morat wasn't against that, but greedy and jealous. He didn't want anyone else to be ... happy. There will be others like him, and won't they be more desperate if they know they'll be ... executed? Instead of having their dissatisfaction heard, and alternatives considered?"

His soft, sweet, kind, little concubine. Who would rise up and fight if she had to. He relished the dichotomy, even as he couldn't grant her this. "I will take counsel on it."

Hurt flashed across her delicate features and she shut her eyes. When she opened them, they were serene—and blank. "Of course. There will be those who can offer insight."

He'd made another mistake in discarding her advice, but he was at a loss. Surely she could understand he knew his people and Meridia best, and would act accordingly? "I would have a conversation with you privately, Celeste."

His parents shifted behind him, as did Bast, and her stare flew to them. "Surely we can talk later, Ruler. I could really use ... the company right now. I never thought I'd see ... anyone I knew here again."

His chest compressed at her request. Yet how might he deny her? He longed to be the only company she desired but had to accept she had closer ties with his first servant and his mother. Their sexual intimacy hadn't forged a bond. *Because I give her only my body and withhold myself.* It was best they return to their original agreement, but he would take better care of her.

Ignoring his inner voice and that nugget of wisdom, he forced another smile and pressed her hand. "Of course. We can talk later. When you're feeling better."

Easing away, he made room for his mother to press forward. Bast rushed to her other side and awkwardly patted her arm. Both spoke quietly to her, expressing their relief and happiness that she was home and relatively unscathed. Lysett took his leave, and his father accompanied him.

"What is wrong between you and your concubine, my son? You haven't moved past the awkward stage as I'd hoped, yet you obviously cherish her. And she you."

"This isn't a conversation for the hall, Father." Numerous guards—loyal ones, he hoped—thronged the corridors, although it was likely to protect against a foe now vanquished. He could accept that he cherished Celeste, for she was beyond price, but could it be possible that she cherished him?

"Then we'll take it to your office," his father announced, forestalling any further consideration.

"I'll join you there. I wish to speak to the healer before he leaves."

He dreaded any conversation about Celeste with his father, but the older man's wisdom had been welcome in the past. As his parent turned in the direction of the office, Lysett called to the healer. Taking him into an alcove, he pitched his voice low.

"Is the royal concubine breeding?" As with Trosan, he knew a pregnancy could be detected by their healers within hours of conception.

"She is not, Ruler. I am perplexed, because there is visible evidence of her fertility, and you have obviously … uh, obviously applied yourself to your duty, but she has not conceived. It is peculiar. But do not lose hope. Other concubines have conceived."

"Perhaps science doesn't always have the answer." His father stood within earshot and Lysett flinched.

Dismissing the healer, he glared at Yu'un and hurried him to the office where they might continue their conversation in private. "Some things are personal."

"Agreed. But these *things*, as you refer to them, are obviously causing you and your concubine considerable angst. It goes past this nonsense with the House of Yehudda. I want to offer my support and any input you might accept."

He decided to ask his own questions first. "What does Mother say? About Celeste?"

"She finds her to be delightful and hold great promise as your mate. There is a reserve, to be expected, yet Ellyce is more concerned about her happiness. Not that your concubine has uttered a word of complaint. But your mother knows not all is well."

"Celeste understands her role, Father."

"And that is?"

"I require heirs. As did you. Our House rules this planet and others. To continue and prevent civil war, I must have a son. Meridia must have children to continue."

"And have you thought past Celeste's role as the vessel for your heirs?"

A warrior's growl built in Lysett's chest as he stared at his sire. His first response was to attack—if only verbally. Except his anger was out of proportion, just as all his reactions in regard to Celeste had been different. With an effort, he composed himself. "She is hardly a mere vessel."

"Exactly. As your mother was not."

"Say what you mean."

"Bast has explained it to you, but perhaps too delicately. So while I haven't interfered for years, I will have my say now, in this matter. Trosan wasn't your match. Oh, the scientists believed they could make it work, but ultimately failed. She was your friend and confidante, wise in the ways of our politics. And her loss won't go unappreciated.

"But as Celeste pointed out, things have changed. What greater of a change is there than joining with another species? You have human males on their way, and I know they aren't coming here to work only in jobs Meridians disdain. And we no longer have slaves. I intuit your reasoning for them coming to live on Meridia. You haven't forgotten our females, some of whom long for a loving union and the blessing of children.

"So I wish to know why you are denying yourself such a thing? And please don't tell me it is out of loyalty to Trosan, who would be the first to box your ears for such misplaced devotion."

Resisting the desire to toss a chair through the window or break his fist on the unforgiving stone wall, Lysett answered. "I don't want to experience such violent and difficult emotions again, Father. If I ensure her safety and don't allow Celeste to connect with me, past giving me heirs, then I can rule and guarantee progress."

"Progress for Meridia. At a cost to yourself. And a greater one for your concubine. A much greater one. How can you not see that?"

Silence reigned, and Lysett blinked past his blurring vision and the pounding of the blood in his head.

He knew the truth when he heard it, as he'd known it despite Bast's station. But could he leave himself open again? He had essentially killed Trosan. And now, Celeste's kidnapping had gutted him. If he let her in and something else happened… It wasn't to be borne.

"I appreciate your wisdom, Father."

With a heavy sigh, Yu'un slapped his hands on his thighs and heaved to his feet. "As I appreciate you hearing me out. Do with it what you will, but think long and hard, son."

As soon as Yu'un left, Lysett went to see Morat. The guard was restrained against the wall in a lower part of the house. The room stank of fear and blood. The male's face bore evidence of several blows, and his clothing was torn, but he'd suffered no real injury.

Morat straightened as much as his binds would allow. "Ruler."

"You've lost the right to be my subject, traitor."

Bowing his head, the male spoke. "I accept my fate."

"Lady Celeste is fine."

Morat's head snapped up. "She is? Oh, that is good."

Desperately wanting to plant his fist in the guard's face, Lysett kept silent, and Morat filled it. "I'm weak. I, too, wanted a concubine and resented those who were given the opportunity. I lost my honor, Sir."

"And you'd deny those who were fortunate."

"To my eternal shame."

"For wealth."

"A poor substitute, but I thought to raise up my family if nothing else."

"At the cost of my concubine's life."

"No!"

"No?"

"The Lady Celeste … it was difficult to find it within myself to dislike her. She is kind and thoughtful, and I heard the talk of her on the ship. She is a fit mate. Yehudda wanted you dead and her as his concubine. It was his mother's last wish."

"His mother was far from dead."

Morat's brow wrinkled and his head tilted in confusion. "I don't understand. He was honoring her last wish. I was to kill you. I won't say I wouldn't have because he insisted on it in order that I claim my reward. But when your concubine prevented me from entering your quarters—I only had the one sensor override—I chose to take her."

Not only had he not protected Celeste, she'd intervened in an assassination attempt on him. Strong emotions gnawed at Lysett's belly. His face must have reflected his inner turmoil because Morat paled, the bruising on his face standing out in stark relief.

He forced himself to urge the other man to continue. "Go on."

"Yehudda was not pleased to learn you were still alive. Not at all. But he accepted Lady Celeste and dismissed me. He said he would offer for her and ask her to refuse you and break your bond."

"He planned to sacrifice her ceremonially. To underscore the unsuitability of taking concubines from another species."

Morat shuddered and visibly swallowed. "I didn't know that at first, Ruler! I swear. Which is why, when I learned of his true plan, I got a message to Bast and opened the gate. I would have done more, but was incapacitated at the outset. I truly believed she would be revered within that House. Quentan was most convincing."

"She was revered *here*."

Morat set his lips and looked everywhere but at Lysett.

"Speak. You've been open thus far."

The other male shook his head and stared at his feet.

"Am I to interpret you disagree? That Lady Celeste is not revered in my house?"

"She is unhappy. She weeps when she thinks no one sees, but I am always there. She caught me watching one time, and I had to pretend I found it distasteful when I wanted to succor her. She suffered. So I had no difficulty taking her to Yehudda." Morat muttered, but the words seemed to echo in the space.

Battered senseless by a man bound to a wall, Lysett strove to keep his wits about him and present an impassive demeanor. When he could trust his voice he asked, "Do you believe I am the source of her unhappiness?" Not that he didn't know the answer.

Morat's brusque nod slammed him in the gut, regardless. The guard blurted, "I hear joyful tales of the other concubines and their chosen. Stories of almost immediate conception."

Silence prevailed for the space of five heartbeats, marred only by the other man's breathing, for Lysett had yet to draw a breath. "You will be taken to the furthest province and stripped of your rank and all your worldly goods. You will suffer the loss of your House's name. You will have no contact with your family—who will not be punished to reflect your perfidy. If you are able to rebuild a life for yourself there, consideration will be given to allowing you to obtain the right to offer for a concubine in the future. But you won't be executed."

"Ruler?" Morat's mouth hung open and his eyes bulged.

"You may thank the Lady Celeste in your

prayers." Lysett strode from the cell with as much decorum as he could manage. It was time he did the right thing, because contrary to more current popular belief, he possessed a modicum of intelligence and insight. He needed to step up.

When he returned to Celeste's room, the door was closed. He was staring at it in resignation when it slid open and Bast crept out. "Ruler!"

"Is she all right?"

"Tired. Shaken up, but fine. She is so resilient. But she regrets damaging the matriarch of that House and I suspect wounding the son preys on her conscience as well. The healer gave her something to help her sleep once she availed herself of nourishment."

"I've banished Morat and wanted to tell her."

"Ah."

"Merely, *ah*, Bast?"

"She believed you would seek counsel about his fate."

"From someone other than herself."

"She accepts she isn't yet an authority on our customs."

"Yet she has diligently studied them so as not to embarrass me. And understands the bigger picture despite her unworldliness."

Bast dipped his head. "She is resilient and adapts. You have foresight and are willing to take the steps, but perhaps you remain rooted in customs that should be modified. Somewhat."

"Seek your bed, Bast. Your years are wearing on you."

"And you, Master?"

"I plan to watch over my concubine."

"As it should be."

Celeste was asleep again, curled up as if to

protect herself. He frowned. She had slept the same way in his bed. There had been nothing to fear then, or so they thought, so… He shook off the introspection. He planned to ensure his concubine had no need to huddle in on herself in the future. The way of it might cut his heart out, but he would do what was ultimately in her best interest.

Carefully tucking the covers around her, he lifted her against his chest and made his way to his quarters. Her bed was too small for the two of them, though he hoped for little space between them tonight. She murmured and cuddled into him and something choked his throat and made it hard to take a deep breath.

Vikte padded nearly silently behind him. Deprived of being part of the assault force while searching Morat's home, he and She-at insisted on taking this shift. She-at lurked on the main floor, in charge of the other guards on post there.

Toting his sweet burden inside his quarters, he waited for the panel to slide shut before placing her on his bed. Then he set another safeguard on the door, preventing anyone from entering unless they blew down the entire wall.

He stripped off and climbed in beside her, calling out for the computer to dim the lights but leave enough to see the surroundings. If Celeste awoke, he wanted her to know exactly where she was. Insinuating his body as close to hers as he could, he shared the bed linens and closed his eyes. It might be the last time he held her, so he was going to indulge himself.

Chapter Thirteen

This wasn't her bed. Had she dreamed that horrible kidnapping? Because she was awake now, rubbing her wrist where she'd pinched herself, and she was most definitely back in Lysett's bed. Dipping her hand beneath the covers, she encountered the fabric of a nightgown and breathed a sigh of relief. At least she told herself it was relief. The back of her was toasty warm, bumped up against a hard—but not uniform—surface. Her hand traveled lower and came across a muscled arm, one that draped loosely over her waist. Her breathing escalated and tears pricked. She couldn't do this. She wasn't ready.

"Good morning." The hard body behind her shifted and the arm tightened a little, drawing her closer.

She was going to cry like a child if she didn't get herself under control. "Morning."

His lips pressed against her hair. She felt the gentle touch as if from a distance as she strove to separate herself. Wiggling in his hold, she gained some space and after a moment, he lifted his arm. She slid to the edge of the bed and set her feet on the floor, the memory of doing much the same thing so recently causing her knees to wobble. She threw a glance at the door.

"It's safeguarded. Nothing will override the system. No one in or out but us. I'll enter your print shortly."

Awkwardly shifting her weight from one foot to the other, she nodded. "Sure. Um, excuse me?"

At his amused nod, those green eyes crinkling at the corners above his rakish stubble, she hustled to the bathing room, sliding the manual door closed. Quickly using the facilities, she washed her hands and threw water on her face. She didn't look as though she'd been through a major event in her life. Not of any kind. The minute signs of the blows Quentan had struck would be indiscernible by tomorrow. And yesterday, before her steady gaze, the healer had confirmed what she suspected. She hadn't conceived. She didn't know whether to be relieved or disappointed, confusion addling her brain. But she learned that conception could be determined instantly with the advanced technology available here.

She had thought she must wait until her body cycled to determine that truth, and it was puzzling that Lysett hadn't told her differently. And had accepted her edict that they not couple again unless necessary. Her first thought was that he'd found their joining morally distasteful and was content to wait. Except he'd come for her two nights ago…

She might have laid awake then and given the situation more consideration, but the tonic pressed on her by the healer had sent her deep into sleep. She'd slept well, with no nightmares and didn't know if it was the medicine or because Lysett had held her all night long.

Unable to make sense of anything, and second-guessing her willingness to give comfort to Lysett—even sexual comfort, she suspected he now felt responsible and guilty for the kidnapping. Or at least for not keeping her safe. Ellyce had indicated as much and Bast didn't disagree. And he'd obviously been worried—and kind— waiting for her to wake after her injuries were healed.

But he hadn't listened, hadn't considered her thoughts on Morat, though humored her. She had to remember her place, and it wasn't anyplace near his level. Maybe he'd put her in his bed because it was the safest place in the house now, though it was like shutting the coop after the fox had run off the chickens. Chickens. Roosters. She shuddered at the visual of Quentan's twisted face and rinsed out her mouth to take away the bad taste.

She hated to go back out there and face Lysett, but he wanted to talk. As far as she was concerned, there was nothing further to say unless he needed reassurance that she didn't blame him for the kidnapping. If he'd been careful with her safety before, she couldn't imagine what it would be like now, what with the chicken coop response and all. She might go as crazy as Quentan. Or his mother. She quashed the vestiges of regret regarding those two, not wanting to dwell on something else she couldn't change. What would *her* mother do? Stroking the necklace, she decided to face him.

With a deep breath, she opened the door and stepped through it. Lysett was still in bed but propped up against the headboard, his broad, muscular chest on display. His bicep flexed as he stretched out his hand and her traitorous eyes were drawn to it. "Come sit with me."

"I'm good." She scooted over to perch on a chair and studied him from across the room.

"Celeste, with what I have to say, I'd appreciate it if you'd sit closer."

Her throat closed off, but she nodded and hesitantly went to him, resolutely keeping her gaze on his instead of taking in all that bare flesh and the way the sheet dipped to mold over his lap. She fought the attraction and willed her arousal away. She couldn't do this with him today, though doubted there would ever be enough time to prepare.

"Yesterday opened my eyes to some things," he began. "Knowing you were at the mercy of a fanatic was indescribable, and the fact you were found safe, or at least not horribly injured—or dead—is something I'll be grateful for, for the rest of my life."

Wow. He took this Ruler position seriously, and she was well aware how the Earth concubine program might turn out if the Rooster had been successful, but he was so subjective. She said as much.

A pained expression tightened Lysett's features and narrowed his eyes. "The ... program ... is secondary. My first concern was for you."

She had nothing to say to that, a wide abyss opening up between her brain and ability to find a coherent thought. He picked up her hand from where it picked nervously at her garment and squeezed it. She tried a smile, still unable to project any words.

"Even so, I denied my feelings once you were home safe, and recovering. I wanted to return to our ... arrangement, telling myself I couldn't tolerate the experience of having harm come to my concubine, again."

"You amended our arrangement. Two nights ago." Her tone was harsh, accusing. Funny how she could speak when he referenced their agreement, but he wasn't playing by the rules. It wasn't fair that he could change them and leave her to deal with the fallout. To hell with his tender feelings.

"I did, and I don't regret it. I don't think you regretted it either."

She bit her lip to contain the bitter things she longed to say in response to his arrogant—and accurate—statement. She contented herself by saying calmly, "Begetting children shouldn't be distasteful, so I'm happy not to regret it."

Lysett flinched. If she'd been sitting in that chair across the room she would have missed it, and she caught her breath. Maybe there was something to those feelings he didn't want to experience. He smiled, but it was a mere lift of those perfectly shaped lips, and it dashed her hope.

"And what if I told you that wasn't about begetting heirs, Celeste?"

On a gasp, she retorted, "Then I would say you are playing a cruel game, far beyond my scope." She didn't know how she felt, then recognized humiliation and despair. *Whore.* Her entire body jumped and she yanked her hand free of Lysett's to cover both ears.

"What's wrong?" He lurched forward and she closed her eyes as the sheet slid lower on his hips. "Celeste. Please."

Regaining a semblance of composure, she folded her hands on her lap, responding to the magic word. "Nothing. I … I suppose I was thinking about yesterday."

"The kidnapping? The way you were treated?"

"Sort of."

"What did he do to you?"

"No more than what you saw. He hit me a few times. Called me names and ranted about me tainting the bloodline. All us concubines. I envisioned far worse."

"I regret even one second of it."

"I know you do. And I don't blame you. Not for any of it." At least they weren't talking about the sex anymore.

"I was sharing my reaction to your ordeal and I fear you are far braver than I."

"Excuse me?"

"It's cowardly to ignore one's feelings and try to hide from them, especially at the expense of another person."

She knew she hid her feelings so as not to cause him grief, but then he wouldn't know that. But he hid from his? Men were different, even her father, who had been a special man. She didn't think she wanted to hear any more from Lysett on the subject. "I'm not sure I understand. Maybe you could take counsel from … someone."

"Ah, to throw my words in my face, Celeste. I deserved that."

"I didn't mean it that way." And she didn't, though yesterday she might have taken some spiteful satisfaction. "I only meant I'm hardly someone you should talk to about ... feelings."

"And who else should I share with, but the person I've been hurting all along?"

Her system couldn't withstand any more shocks. Not one more. He couldn't know he was hurting her. She had her pride and it had to take her forward. "You don't need to think that way. I'm fine. Fine. I accepted your terms. We should just … carry on."

"Those around us have ascertained your unhappiness. Are you saying you *are* happy?"

Lord, he was relentless. Who were these people who thought her unhappy? And why should he care? Unless he was stuck on his lapse in protecting her. So confusing. She was back in his home, unharmed, and presumably still fertile, if not yet pregnant. What more did he want from her, unless he was planning to release her from the agreement?

Her vision swam and her belly clenched. That was it. She was being sent back to the dorm, away from him. Being replaced. All because she hadn't effectively faked being happy. She'd settle for half a loaf if it meant spending even a little time with Lysett, no matter that made her pathetic. The thought of him with another woman… She found herself babbling, "I'm happy. Very happy. Why wouldn't I be happy? My life here is far superior to that on Earth. I have everything someone like me could hope for. Are you sending me back?" *Whore.*

She blinked at the auditory hallucination and only just managed not to stick her fingers in her ears. She couldn't block out the truth.

Lysett looked terribly serious and concerned. His eyes were soft and he reached for her hands again. "I can't keep you if I can't make you happy, Celeste. I have to do the right thing."

She heard *I can't keep you*. Numbness worked its way down from the back of her nose, past her throat, to seize her chest. She couldn't make her lungs work.

"Your hands are cold. You're shaking. Celeste?"

Blame it on being stolen from her planet and conveyed to an entirely different world, failing to measure up for its Ruler, then being betrayed by her guard, taken by a madman and threatened with a gruesome death, and finally rejected in totality by a man she'd stupidly fallen in love with... Blame it on anything ... but she couldn't keep it together. Not for another instant. Yanking free of his grasp, she crumpled and curled into a ball, a deluge of tears falling to scald her cheeks, sobs and shallow cries tearing at the back of her throat.

Dragged onto Lysett's lap and wrapped securely in his arms merely exacerbated her anguish. Celeste choked for air and made ineffective efforts to escape his hold. He shushed her and rubbed her back, and finally she focused on the steady beat of his heart to bring herself back under control. She'd accepted her lot stoically for much of life and now she'd let it all out and humiliated herself in front of the Ruler, so it was time to move on. She just needed a minute.

He tucked a finger under her chin and urged her head up. Staring at her face, he worked his thumbs across her cheeks to brush the tears away. She tried to interpret whatever stood in his eyes before catching the thought and discarding it. Fooling herself was especially self-flagellating and stupid. She sniffled and knew she was a total mess. Lysett passed her what she'd have called a handkerchief back on Earth and she blew her nose and mopped up as best she could. He stroked her hair off of her brow and tightened his hands around her waist.

"How is it that while I feel so protective of you in this moment and wish to take your pain away, that I also require you? Badly."

She shifted on his lap, becoming aware of him hardening beneath her hip, and understood it was lust she'd seen simmering in his green orbs. Empty and lost from her emotional storm, she didn't fight the arousal his masculine appreciation drew from her, as he slid his hands to cup her buttocks. *Half a loaf.* He urged her to her knees, to straddle him, and she allowed him to manipulate her body, carried along on a wave of need. Anything to ground her and leave her with a memory to ease her in the years to come.

Her nightgown inched upward before his questing fingers, and she shuddered when her exposed inner thighs slid along his hips, her knees spread impossibly wide. Lysett's stare remained intently on her face, and she looked back, blearily committing his features in her mind until the fabric skirted her shoulders and blinded her, lifting over her head.

When he tossed the garment aside, she blinked and watched as his gaze dropped to her chest. Her nipples pebbled, but not from a chill. Leaning forward, he touched her mother's necklace with one finger, then kissed the upper slopes of her breasts, first one, then the other, and set his lips in the valley of her cleavage. A gentle pressure, she soaked it in and let her head fall back. She needed him so badly.

"Your heart beats quickly, Celeste. Say you need

this. Say you want me."

As a farewell, it should smack of tawdriness, but she had no will to dissect her reasoning, and nor did she want to concern herself with his. "I want you." *I need you. I love you.*

She was beneath him in the next breath, his broad shoulders blocking the view of anything but him. Golden skin stretched over planes of muscle and long bones and she feasted on the visual. He crouched over her, and reverently cupped her breasts. His thumbs feathered over the bunched tips and sent shivers of anticipation throughout her being. Her center liquefied, her folds dampening in preparation as his mouth enveloped a nipple, suckling and lashing it with his tongue.

Tiny cries slipped past her lips and she worked her fingers through his hair to press him closer, ignoring any expectation she remain passive. "Please."

Moving to her neglected breast, he laved it while cupping the one he abandoned, the moisture he'd left behind cooling as it dried. Inundated with sensation, she writhed and tugged at his hair, then lifted against his wide erection.

"You're ready for me? So soon?"

She'd always be ready for him, and the shame of it washed away before the flood of her arousal. "Please."

"Soon, my concubine."

Trailing kisses over her belly, he worked his way over her mound. Losing her grip on his hair, her fingertips pattered against the sheet, seeking something to anchor herself. When he reached his goal and settled between her legs to tantalize and torture her with long, languid licks of her folds, she whimpered and pleaded until he focused attention on the nub of her sex.

Her release built slowly but inexorably, ripples of sensation that spread to encompass her entire body, and she let it take her, shuddering through the powerful climax. Lysett petted her gently as she settled and collapsed in a boneless splay of limbs.

"I treasure your surrender to me, Celeste." He covered her body with his, and she soaked in his heat, content to simply feel because she had the rest of her life for recriminations.

The now familiar weight of him settled between her thighs and effectively immobilized her, not that she would deny him. Not now. His hard length slid between her folds and notched at her opening.

"Look at me, Celeste."

She met his stare as he advanced between her orgasm-swollen tissues. The intimacy was excruciatingly painful and she closed her eyes in self-defence. Fully sheathed in her body, he lowered until she could feel his breath by her temple as he murmured words the translator didn't interpret. She bit her lip and swallowed the things she longed to tell him, holding him tightly to her instead. Her fingers splayed over his smooth back and coasted over the divots of his spine.

His measured thrusts drove her toward another climax, a mellow, contented sensation as she rocked to meet him. *I love you.* His groan melded with her silent admission, and in that moment she pretended it was Lysett who'd professed his love as he flooded her with his seed. If this was goodbye, at least she'd joined with him acknowledging the love in her heart.

He stilled and kissed her shoulder, and then her jaw, his dark, silky hair stroking her face. A solitary tear squeezed from one eye, despite her best efforts to contain it, and meandered down to meet his lips. She felt him tense.

His quiet words were delivered without any appreciable emotion as he withdrew and put some space between them. She was instantly chilled and oh, so empty. "Forgive me. Males express themselves physically. Or attempt to. I—"

She looked everywhere but at him, and hitched onto her side to maintain her precious memory. Already it was fleeting. He cut his words off and drifted a covering over her. She snuggled into it for comfort.

"I will make the appropriate arrangements for the morning, Celeste."

The lights dimmed further and she stared blindly into the darkness, feeling him settle behind her but at such a distance. She wondered what a single female Earther could do on Meridia as she'd never be a concubine again. Or if she would have to return to Earth. Best she focus on her fate instead of the status of her broken heart.

****

He waited for sleep to claim him, incredibly aware of the proximity of his concubine. He longed to draw her close and hold her while she slept. Except she wasn't his, not anymore, and what kind of male was he that he'd used his influence to join with her this one last time? Had he truly believed he could heal her emotional wounds with physical pleasure and in doing so tell her how he felt? He hadn't the courage to tell her what he'd only just allowed himself to accept, until right the point of his extremis. *I love you.* And she hadn't responded...

That one shimmering tear reinforced his decision. He had to do what was right for her, and *he* clearly wasn't. Celeste deserved someone who could make her happy.

Realizing that sleep would continue to elude him, he eased out of bed and padded to his dresser, using the ambient light from his tablet to guide him. Bast would be awake. His first servant prided himself on requiring little sleep, and would be toiling on a public information release prior to the presentation. He hesitated. There need be no presentation. He was in no state of mind to choose another concubine, even supposing there might be another suitable for his House.

Duty be damned. He wanted Celeste. But this wasn't about what he wanted. If she was breeding, he might have been able to look past his noble intention to free her, because motherhood might make her happy. And at least he could see her every day. But there had been be no progeny from their joining, and this détente couldn't continue.

Snatching up his tablet, he sent a message to Bast and tossed the device back down as if it burned his fingers. He drew on the first pieces of clothing his hands fumbled upon and lowered himself to the chair where Celeste had perched before he'd seduced her. Leaning back, he resigned himself to many long hours before the new day. He took comfort in knowing his concubine was at least safe, and in the days that followed, she might find her happiness.

Chapter Fourteen

She drifted around the nice, little personal space Bast had arranged for her. If she focused on the minutiae of the present, she could pretend she hadn't been escorted with grave courtesy to her former quarters in the Ruler's home by the man himself and left there to assemble her belongings. She couldn't even really recall the pretty speech he'd made.

"Bast will see to your resettlement and ensure you have everything you require, Celeste. I want you to know that I regret causing you a hint of discomfort, let alone the way I treated you, out of misplaced entitlement. My actions reflect poorly on my House and I wish I had handled things differently. You have my deepest apologies."

He had looked totally sincere, too, and worryingly tired, his handsome features drawn and strained. Even his eyes had lost their luster. But she wasn't a *thing* to be handled differently, and no longer cared much about any*thing*. She had nodded to convey her acceptance and understanding, and he'd made an awkward movement, as though to reach for her, before turning on his heel and stalking in true Ruler fashion out the door. And out of her life.

But she didn't actually remember any of that because only fools tortured themselves.

A throat clearing caused her to turn to face the young male Meridian peering into her room. "Lady Celeste?"

"Yes?"

"Lady Shirley and Lady Belinda are here."

It had been weeks. Bast insisted that none of the concubines were allowed to be out and about because of a surprising piece of news. Well, surprising to her and the majority, she supposed. A few hundred Earth males had landed on Meridia, traveling on smaller vessels, like the one she'd first boarded—had been carried aboard. The Ruler had also taken into consideration Meridia's single females and invited human males to relocate with a view to finding a mate. The fact he had adapted his approach likely proved he was indeed ruling material, and she recalled his contention to reach out to Earth to invite additional females here. Not that she'd be required to play a role in that any longer—a very good thing.

In any event, caution was the watchword. The integration of the human males was similar to that of the females, but for fear it would stir up dormant purists, all concubines were placed under house protection in the interim. It made good sense, although she'd missed her friends. But now that they were here, she knew they'd threaten her brittle composure. She pasted on a wide smile and moved to the door. "Lead on, Jaycob."

There were several guards situated in the building where she and a few other unplaced concubines resided. She'd heard the warriors' number had increased two-fold and supposed that was because of her and her previous royal connections. Safeguarding was only reasonable, at least until it was certain the resistance had been rooted out. She marked their commanding figures and looked in their faces as she passed by, wondering if there was another Morat within their ranks.

In truth, she wasn't really concerned, but as she obviously had no skill in detecting the true person behind the façade, had fallen into the habit of putting names to faces. Almost all of them gave her a friendly, if reserved, nod. But then, so had Morat.

"Celeste!" Shirley rushed forward, Belinda close behind. Her fellow humans looked … radiant. Actually glowing. She absorbed it as if from a great distance, not wishing to get burned.

"It's good to see you."

"Bullshit." Belinda hadn't developed any nicety of mannerisms, and Celeste liked that. Some things stayed the same.

"I *am* glad to see you. The other concubines stay away from me like I'm carrying a plague."

"Probably just intimidated."

Or worried I'll taint their hopes for a good match. "Maybe."

Shirley wrapped an arm around her waist. "What happened? Why did you refuse the Ruler?"

That was the story floating around. She supposed she should be grateful that she had been painted as the spurner instead of the spurnee, but, with the exception of the guards who affected those stoic masks, people tended to look at her as if she was deranged. How could she have thrown such a chance away? She shrugged. She didn't care if they knew the truth that she didn't measure up, but it was evidently important to the Ruler and he knew his politics.

"I wasn't happy." That was the truth, too.

"We're not happy all the time," Shirley protested.

"Bullshit." It was worth the profanity to see her friends' faces blank in shock. "You both look … like you're well loved."

Shirley nodded and Belinda actually blushed.

"But you knew that early on, Celeste," Shirley said. "I told you on our last visit—the one where you promised you were going to call me."

She'd been a little busy, fielding the mixed messages from the Ruler—no more *Lysett*—and getting kidnapped and all. "Well, we're together now, and you can come see me as often as you like."

"And you can come to visit me."

"And me."

And see them together with their males? Probably not. At least not for a while. Like a few years. Decades. She didn't need any additional reminders of what she'd never had, or would be likely to have. Apparently there was a certain cachet to obtaining her favor, a male being able to replace the Ruler as it were, but she had absolutely no interest in fueling that thought. She nodded and led them to her room.

"It's perfect for you." Shirley gawked much as she had in the Ruler's abode.

"I like it. Bast arranged it. And of course, I have the rest of the complex for anything else I need. Clothing. Meals." Though she didn't go to the dining room anymore. Sitting alone with a crowd of women a few tables over, talking about her, got old fast.

Belinda plopped down on a comfortable chair. "Ash got me a beautiful dress for the presentation. And now there won't be one." She mock-scowled at Celeste.

"Then you'll have to tease him into taking you somewhere else to wear it." She wondered how she'd tossed the words out, because she had assumed the Ruler would work fast and choose one of the women not yet mated, and it haunted her. That's why she went to the dining room at first, to count noses, but the numbers hadn't diminished. But that didn't mean there weren't others in different places for him to check out. "I imagine there will be one in the future."

"You're really okay with it." Shirley peered at her as if trying to see into her soul.

"I refused, remember?"

"Okay, honey, but if you need to talk…"

"Sure. Now, tell me what's new." If she talked about it, she'd have to figure out a way to cope all over again.

"I'm pregnant. No longer a suspicion!"

"Me, too."

In a kinder world, she might have said *me three*, and a pang of anguish lanced through her fabricated serenity. "I'm so happy for you." And she was. She *could* be happy for this.

"I hear many of the matches have resulted in conception. Ash is hovering like he's accomplished the most remarkable thing ever. And I suppose he has." Belinda pressed her hand against her belly. "I was as surprised as anything, seeing as I figured it was just lust."

"Excuse me?"

The other woman chuckled and Shirley wiggled her eyebrows in a comical fashion as Belinda continued, "I liked the guy, even after I found out he was chosen by the Ruler to be the Liaison with Earth. In charge of our … removal from home. He's really good-looking and has that arrogant thing working for him so I was fine with giving it a go. I mean, I was here and figured there was nothing back home. And the sex is great, but turns out there's a lot more. We're making history."

Shirley chimed in, "The healers are checking historical data, and natural conception is believed to occur only if a bond develops."

"You can use the real 'L' word," Belinda teased. "I'm not that cynical anymore."

"So … desire … lust … isn't enough to procreate." Celeste tried to make sense of it. The anguish returned, full force, and she couldn't even say *make a baby*.

"Nope. And all the monkeying around the scientists did to orchestrate pregnancies wasn't successful because the aphrodisiac created fake desire … and apparently there's no substitute for love. Those offspring couldn't be viable, and the mothers paid a terrible price, but it seems they're only now figuring it out."

Had the Ruler known that interesting tidbit when he returned her like … damaged goods? "How did you find all of this out?"

Shirley dug her tablet out of a bag that hung loosely from her wrist. "It's all in here. Just released." She scrolled through a feed. "It puts a different face on bringing all of us here to Meridia, I think. You know. Developing a bond, falling in love. It takes it out of the *propagating the species* realm of thought. Makes it harder for the naysayers to make a case against us."

"It's nice not to be prostituting myself," Belinda agreed cheerfully. "I'm head over heels, and so is Ash."

Celeste thought her face might crack beneath the interested look and smile she grimly kept painted on for the duration of the visit. The conversation turned to babies and names and finally discussion about more mundane matters. She contributed through numb lips when she detected the need to respond. The Ruler had dodged a bullet although he hadn't minded the practice sessions. Neither had she, and what did that make her? She didn't need the Rooster her to call her names.

Her friends departed with promises to return soon and repeated invitations to their homes. She parried the latter and tried to be positive about the former, and nearly collapsed with relief once they left and she could close herself in her room.

Bodily needs drove her from her bed, from where she sought fitful slumber and thought about exactly nothing, catching her thoughts when they veered in unacceptable directions. Once she was up, her body aching from inactivity, she decided to request a tray. She didn't have the inclination to even visit an empty dining room, though avoiding the other unmatched concubines would be easier as it wasn't a normal meal time. She supposed they'd heard of the new study, and wondered what they would make of it. Did some of them have romantic dreams?

The same young male presented the food with his usual deference.

"Thank you, Jaycob."

"Bast has requested that you receive him."

She'd ignored the repeated pinging of her tablet while she moped. "When did he make the request?"

"Nearly two days ago. I ... I advised him you weren't feeling well and wished to be undisturbed. I'm not sure that was the right thing to do."

"It was absolutely the right thing," she assured him and then intuited his muted concern. "The Ruler's first servant finds it difficult to be denied, but he agreed to your role here and must observe it."

"I am honored to be your gatekeeper, Lady Celeste. Are you feeling better?"

"Yes." She wasn't, not really. The long rest hadn't helped her recover her equilibrium, and the idea of food now repelled her.

"Shall I contact Bast?"

"I'll do it," she promised, and he looked vastly relieved as he exited.

In the end, all she could manage was the tea. Everything else on the tray exuded strange smells, and she found herself longing for a plate of roasted turnip. With a garnish of green pepper. Both of which she'd grown in her garden plot on Earth. *Must be homesickness.*

Shoving the food aside, she contacted Bast, who was reproachful in that subtle manner he wielded so effectively. Feeling guilty, she agreed to see him at the evening meal and counted herself lucky that she hadn't lost him, too. Not that she'd ever had his master.

She picked through her clothing, having left the bulk of the Ruler's largesse in her rooms there. She didn't want to wear anything from that time. There weren't a lot of choices, but she chose a dark-blue gown, thinking it would complement her the best until she caught sight of her wan face and the dark circles under her eyes. Maybe she *was* ill, the fatigue and uneasy belly symptoms of something more ominous than a broken heart. She laughed out loud at her ridiculous musing, but it came out as broken pieces of sound.

If she didn't feel better tomorrow, she'd ask Jaycob to request that a healer attend her. Her hand froze in midair, the hairbrush slipping from her numb fingers when an incredulous thought surfaced. Fumbling for her tablet, she called up a calendar and tapped through the days. She did it once. Twice. And again. She should have cycled shortly after that horrible day with crazy Quentan. The healer told her she wasn't pregnant—not breeding, then.

But she'd greedily coupled with Lysett shortly thereafter... Some times were more fertile than others, but... She carefully set the tablet down, lest it suffer the same fate as her brush, and requested the information Shirley had shared about the new discovery regarding procreation. Reading it carefully from beginning to end, she took a sobbing breath. There had to be a bond. Both parties had to love the other. Both. So she wasn't pregnant. Whatever was wrong with her, she hoped it wasn't a strange alien disease that had escaped the inoculations all the prospective concubines received on the ship prior to landing.

Smoothing her dress, she sat to wait for Bast's arrival. They'd spend a pleasant hour and he'd speak to her as an equal and catch her up on all the doings on Meridia. The Ruler's name wouldn't come up except as he related to what Bast had to share, and she made a mental note to ask after Lady Ellyce and Yu'un. The nice woman wanted to visit, but appearances must be upheld for the time being, and it had been difficult to converse with her via the video link. At least on Celeste's part. Ellyce had been nothing but kind and somehow refrained from asking all the obvious questions. But Celeste knew their friendship would peter out.

****

"She isn't well. Jaycob guards her privacy fiercely and is intensely loyal, so it's difficult for me to breach that protection, considering that I set it up myself," Bast advised. "But other than long walks around the perimeter gardens, she keeps to herself, and of late stays confined to her room more frequently. She is thinner and very pale, even for a human. If the amount she eats is reflected by how much she consumes when I join her for a meal … well, she barely ingests enough for a bird."

Lysett wasn't feeling well himself, and hearing that Celeste was ill… "Has she seen a healer?"

"She agreed to contact one. I believe she is a trifle concerned that she's contracted something here despite the inoculations."

"Send my personal healer. Immediately."

"The one you won't see yourself?"

"I'm fine."

"You pine for her." Bast blithely overstepped his boundaries, as he'd done for some time, but Lysett had no energy to pretend. His parents were also concerned—for both him and Celeste—but accepted his explanation that he'd made her terribly unhappy and she didn't feel the same way about him as he did about her.

"I've gone through this before." *And I'm not doing it again. Ever. Duty be damned.* "I'll survive it."

"You were profoundly guilty and saddened over Trosan, Master. This is different."

How could he give voice to the emptiness? The loss? It was as if half his soul was absent, and he was wasting away. Different indeed. Immeasurably worse, because Celeste wasn't physically beyond his reach... He kept going only because he'd done the right thing and he had to rule.

"Once she is healthy, Celeste will find her joy in life. You will assist her in the path she wants to travel." He couldn't think about her bonding with another male, preferring to fool himself with thoughts of her doing other things that would make her happy. Anything.

"She may choose to return to Earth."

That idea gutted him, though not ever seeing her again might be for the best. "She may."

"She is definitely not happy at the moment. She was better off here."

Lysett shoved back from the desk, sending his chair into the wall. "She was miserable here. She cried. Many saw it, including you. Being my concubine was the worst choice for her. Don't presume to question my decision." The Goddess knew he questioned it enough for any and all doubters.

His first servant ducked his head. "I apologize, Master. I simply feel we have overlooked something important."

"She doesn't return my ... regard. I kept her here against her will by deciding as royal concubine she could not refuse. I made a grave error and now we must give her time."

Bast spoke under his breath but Lysett heard him. *Regard.*

"Don't censor your voice now, Bast. It's too late for that."

"I was merely wondering if *regard* translated into *love*, Ruler."

"As you say." Although he'd never say it. At least not out loud, again. He'd sooner have his organs carved out of his body, not that it could hurt more than his chest. His longing for Celeste would surely pass, or at least dwindle if he didn't say he words.

"I'll send the healer."

****

"Impossible." If she hadn't been lying down, she'd be on the floor. Celeste stared in horror at the healer's beaming visage.

"My instruments do not lie. I checked twice. You have conceived. Your child is three weeks and a few days in development."

"But I read the study. Your name is on it. The one about love, bonding, and procreation."

His face clouded. "This is perplexing. You are here because you used your right to refuse, I understand." He peered at her. "The child *is* our Ruler's?"

"What? Of course, it is. You can't tell with your *instrument*?" This couldn't be happening. His inference made her want to slap him. She might have traded her body for survival, but she'd only done it for one man.

"I didn't search the DNA. I didn't think it necessary until you raised the question of the study."

She was blaming the messenger, but how many times could a person be so sorely tested? "Could a child be conceived if only one party … is in love? Was in love?"

The healer shook his head emphatically, his long hair swaying in time. "No. The sampling doesn't lie. The hormones and the brain waves concur. It equates the love matches in our history and the offspring that were produced. We Meridians disdained deeper emotions in favor of conquest and proceeds and paid a terrible price. It is a most unscientific finding in that regard." Another wide smile lightened his face. "Love is a difficult thing to measure, but it has prevailed."

"I must be an anomaly."

"You would be the first."

"But it is possible."

"Possible, but not probable. In fact, the odds are definitely against it. We need to consult with the Ruler."

"No!"

"I do not know what the ethics of your world, Lady Celeste, but is it customary for females to hide conception from the male?"

"Sometimes."

"I cannot understand that. Children are a joyful event. Surely human males are pleased?"

"That's not the only reason."

"Perhaps you can explain."

She crossed the room and stared out the window. "Life is hard on Earth. Having another mouth to feed is difficult—"

"But not here."

Whirling, she glared at him, really wanting to shoot the messenger. "Do you want to know the reasons or not?"

"Only if they pertain to the Ruler."

Well, that drew the fight out of her. The old man would be horrified if she compared his master to some human males who ran out on the women they'd impregnated or treated them badly because of the pregnancy. Or worse, were cruel to the child. She knew it happened, more than the ones who were happy to have a child, but a Meridian would never understand that.

Obviously they had come to appreciate what they'd so blithely passed over in favor of what the healer had termed material things.

Returning to sit with him, she tried again, searching for a way out, refusing to consider that damned study because hope would kill her. "I'd like to talk to Bast."

Eyes narrowing, the healer drew up to his full height. "May I inquire why?"

Lord, he thought Bast was the father. A surge of inappropriate laughter welled up and she let it out. When it reduced her to sobs, the male awkwardly patted her shoulder. "Would you have the first servant tell his master?" he asked.

She wanted to tell him *yes*. It was the coward's way out, but Celeste had visions of the Ruler discounting the medical tests and doing whatever was done to women who accused him of making them pregnant. Except that didn't take place here. She choked back more laughter, then sobered, wondering if something might have happened with Quentan when she was unconscious.

"Wait. Could that Quentan have—?"

"No, Lady Celeste. I assure you. I examined you after that time. Your child was conceived in love. Bast must tell the Ruler of his perfidy, of course. But we will come to some accord. My Master will not like the news, but he will support a union because of the child."

"Bast is not the father." She wanted to smack the man. Again. "But I'd rather he tell your master."

"Allow me to test for paternity."

She could hardly say no. "Fine."

The instrument didn't feel like anything when it pressed against her abdomen, but it garnered information that the old man sifted through. "The child is indeed the Ruler's."

"I told you."

Shaking his head, the healer said, "I don't understand. This is all highly irregular." His face cleared. "Is this a lover's spat?"

"What?"

"A lover's spat. We have recovered some of old Earth's vernacular."

Well, she and the Ruler had been lovers. Just not *in* love, at least on his side. She wasn't sure about the spat part, but it sounded vile enough. "That's it. A spat."

"Then you have nothing to be concerned about. He is a good man and this will cheer him up and make him well again."

She found herself almost in the old man's face, worried sick. "What's wrong with him?"

"Fatigue and depression. He hasn't been himself since you refused him."

"I didn't—" She was tired of dancing around with the healer. He seemed to be talking on an entirely different level and she was sick of trying to decipher everything. She was glad Lysett wasn't really ill, though she didn't like the sound of it.

After a few moments, presumably giving her time to complete her statement, the old man said, "I will alert Bast to set a time for you and the Ruler to meet. You can share the good news."

Or I will tell him. The unspoken warning hung in the ensuing silence.

The healer didn't have to say it, didn't have to voice the inevitable, but *she* was having the last word. "Your master can come here."

"But—"

"Here." She was going to have the sanctuary of her nice little room to retreat to when the proverbial crap hit the fan—more old Earth vernacular—and would not meet the Ruler on his own territory. Not that the whole planet didn't belong to him in some fashion, but still…

"I will ask him to come at once."

"Fine."

Stamping down on a flicker she blamed on hormones and not hope, she hurried to freshen up and called for Jaycob to open a room across from hers so she didn't have far to flee. Maybe she could write Lysett a note and hand it to him while she waited by the door for him to read it. She could have a head start. Instead, she rehearsed a few lines in her head and resolved to get it over and done with as quickly as possible. Seeing him again would be like ripping the bandage off a horrid wound.

She didn't even have time to change her dress before Jaycob was signaling at her door.

"He is here, Lady Celeste. Waiting." The young male didn't wring his hands, but she thought he wanted to.

"I'm coming. Thank you."

"I'll send up refreshments."

"No need, Jaycob." Touching her necklace for inspiration, she mustered her courage and her feet carried her forward.

Lysett was pacing the room Jaycob had chosen, a large, nearly empty space with only a large couch, a couple of chairs and some small tables grouped together. It made for an intimate discussion or gave a person room to move around freely.

As soon as she slipped inside, Lysett moved to her, his face a study of worry and concern. Her heart seized at the raw emotion and she noted how truly exhausted he appeared. The healer hadn't exaggerated.

She tried to greet him, to ask him how he was, when he touched her, clutching her shoulders in his big hands, and the words died on her lips. Bending, he peered into her eyes. "What is wrong, Celeste? The healer told me I was to come to you immediately but insisted you tell me the reason yourself. Here, come and sit."

Allowing him to draw her to the couch, she plopped down and sought her rehearsed statements. He forestalled her, wrapping one arm around her waist and arranging her on his lap. His broad chest heaved and he nestled his face against her hair. His voice broke as he spoke, "I don't think I can stand to hear it from your lips. Better the healer tell me."

"Sir. Ruler—" He was so tense and a fine tremor shuddered through his big frame. She badly wanted to comfort him and somehow worked her arms free to ease around his shoulders. Holding him closely, she shushed him like a child and stroked the back of his neck. This wasn't sex, so she didn't have to be passive. Did she?

His sex stirred against her buttocks and she froze and carefully shifted away. Lysett choked out a strangled laugh and raised his head. She reluctantly loosened her grip and met his stare. The roiling emotion reflected back made her blink.

"I fear you are going to tell me the worst possible news, that you are dying, and yet I become aroused. No wonder you don't return my feelings. I disgust even myself."

"I'm not dying." She could at least say that, unable to process the rest.

"Thank the Goddess." He shut his eyes tightly and sucked in a great draft of air through his nose.

"What ... what feelings?" It was probably the stupidest question she would ever ask, and she was leaving herself wide open for another gut-wrenching experience, but she had to ask it. Maybe she should have asked it before, weeks ago, when he'd made that incomprehensible reference to them.

"I swore I wouldn't say it again. Not when you didn't acknowledge me. But then why would you, when I'd seduced you yet again? Used my status with you to entice your surrender."

Maybe everybody on this planet was some kind of crazy. Or she was, and thinking she was the only sane one. "What are you talking about?"

A touch of the old arrogant Lysett presented itself. He stiffened—and not just the piece of anatomy against her hip—and looked down his nose at her. "For a mere slip of an Earther, you test me more than anyone I know. Is this my punishment for disallowing your refusal when you were within your rights to do so?"

"Did you make that up? That "no right to refuse a royal" thing?" She knew she was getting sidetracked, but she embraced the hint of anger. Far better than the anguish he'd caused.

"It was an old custom but rarely implemented, if ever."

"So why did you pull it on me?"

His gorgeous mouth tightened and she feared she had pushed too hard, but with a sigh, he answered, "Because I couldn't let you get away."

Okay. Okay. She said, cautiously, "There were other concubines."

"They weren't you."

"What's so special about me?"

"Everything. I simply couldn't accept it at the time but knew I couldn't allow you to leave and seek another match. I did know that much when I wasn't focusing on my duty."

"So what happened? Please tell me."

"I finally accepted what I feel for you…" He

frowned. "This is more difficult than facing a squad of the enemy, Celeste, but perhaps you will understand and come to forgive me in time. I owe you that. I accepted I had fallen in love with you, and I used my rank to try and keep you."

Knowing he waited for some response, maybe even a gracious platitude, didn't kick-start her brain. He'd fallen in love with her, kept her at arm's length, and made her miserable because he couldn't acknowledge it? All of that should matter, and make her furious, and it did. But it didn't. "Do you still feel that way?"

"Our time apart has tormented me. But I didn't make you happy and how could you come to love me? So I did the right thing and let you go. I haven't done anything more difficult in my life, but I finally did it. But enough about that. Celeste, what is wrong? Why are you ill? What does the healer say?"

"Your subjects had better not find out how lacking you are in your private life."

He stood her between his knees in a mind-boggling display of strength, hands gripping her upper arms. Their faces were on the same level and the heat of anger and humiliation colored his face a faint red beneath the golden skin. His eyes sparked, and she shoved forward to press her lips against his mouth. He opened in surprise and she slipped her tongue inside to flirt with his, drinking in his taste.

Lysett assumed control immediately and deepened the kiss, devouring her mouth and stealing her breath until she went lax. Immediately, he drew back and cupped her face in one big hand. "What are you doing, Celeste?"

Filling her lungs, she croaked, "You need to find a way to use that political savvy of yours. Find the way with words that helps you rule a universe, and use it in your personal relationships. Our relationship. You should have told me that you loved me!"

Dropping his head, he shook it slowly from side to side. "I did."

"When?"

"The last time we joined."

"Was that you?"

His head shot up, and one eyebrow quirked. "Who else was there?"

"I thought *I* said it. I mean, I thought it."

His throat worked against a swallow, and a hint of perspiration dotted his upper lip. "I had hoped you felt that way, but it was me who said it. And I meant it."

"You were right in your hope, and I should have said it because I feel it."

"Say it now. Please."

"I love you, Ruler."

"Lysett."

"Oh." Her wide smile made her face hurt in a good way. He was giving her permission to be familiar and any doubts she had slipped away. "I love you, Lysett."

"And I love you, Celeste, my concubine. You *are* still my concubine?" He probably never sounded vulnerable, and she didn't think she ever wanted to hear it in his voice again, but she cherished it now. And would take care of him.

"I am. And I always will be."

"Was I a fool, then?"

"Maybe. But you're always going to communicate from here on, so it shouldn't be a big problem."

Wry humor glinted in his eyes. "My father didn't rule my mother either."

"I like your parents and I believe they like me. I

think they'll be happy for us."

"They've liked you better than me this past while, but that's a story I'm sure they'll tell you over and over in the future." His face tightened. "How long before you will be well? You haven't told me what the healer said?"

"I should be back to normal in about eight months, give or take a few days. Nothing too much to worry about, as it's something most human women experience. Although you can expect some mood swings and weight gain and such."

Every hint of color drained from his face, his emerald eyes blazing as he deciphered her riddle. His hands softened on her and quivered. His lips parted, then closed. "I... Two blessings in such a short space of time. Celeste..."

She cuddled close and he wrapped her up again, sheltering her against his chest. The heat of him unraveled her. "You've never disgusted me, you know," she whispered. "And I don't think you have to quit seducing me just because I'm pregnant. We need to practice for the next one."

Chapter Fifteen

"You look spectacular." Shirley scanned her from head to toe. "That dress is perfect. So rich and … and sexy. But regal. You took a long time to get there, but you're the Ruler's mate. It's written all over you. Everyone here can see it."

The room was full of human females and their mates, with a few human males escorting Meridian females showing up here and there. That process was going well, if a bit slower. Celeste scanned the space before smiling at Shirley. "Thanks. Mother Ellyce helped me pick it out, but I wasn't sure that it suited me at first."

"It's such a rich brown and it fits you beautifully."

She'd decided to eschew the heavy jewelry Ellyce had offered her, preferring to wear her mother's necklace. An image of Lysett nestled beside that of her family, and Celeste couldn't ask for anything more.

"You look pretty good yourself." And her friend did, in a dark-green dress that set off her coloring.

Shirley beamed and ran a hand over her belly. "This baby is agreeing with me. Poor Belinda, she's had some morning sickness, but that didn't keep her away tonight. She had to wear that scarlet gown someplace."

Belinda stood out like a flame, her mate's dark head ducked close to her red one as she laughed up at him. Celeste didn't think her heart could get any fuller, but seeing so many happy couples made it overflow. And most were indeed pregnant. She hoped the medical community was prepared for a wealth of babies all around the same time.

Mother Ellyce stepped up and hugged her, nodding cordially to Shirley. "Are you well, my dear? Is this too much for you?"

"I feel fine. Lysett hovers and frets until I could scream, you know."

"I'll take the hint, Celeste." Ellyce smiled from ear to ear. "But you must take the greatest care."

"I have months to go, but every healer report is positive. There haven't been any red flags with any of the concubines, you know. We're all healthy stock and well taken care of. It's not like Earth."

Shirley said, "I doubt half of us would have had children without difficulties if we were still there."

Ellyce nodded. "The risks on Earth are significant, I know that. So it's good you're here. It will take time before we Meridians become accustomed to not continually worrying about our mothers-to-be."

"Sooner than later, I hope, Mother Ellyce." Celeste patted her arm. "I can't imagine how difficult it was."

"You are important to us, Celeste." Ellyce looked weepy and Celeste wanted to cry a little too. Hormones. Shirley blinked madly.

"Mother, you'll have the entire hall in tears." Lysett, never far, had been conversing with a member of another high-ranking House while she and Shirley visited. But he didn't miss anything where she was concerned. She relished the way he tucked her up against his side and leaned in close to him.

"Such a joyous occasion, son." Ellyce dashed a fingertip past the corner of one eye and slipped away with a smile.

"You are well?" Lysett set her away from him slightly and scanned her, focusing in on her eyes.

"I'm fine. Tired, but that's to be expected, apparently."

His green eyes flared and he pulled her close.

Lips close to her temple, he murmured, "This gown is provocative, but only at times. It hints at your secret passion and I can't keep my eyes off of you."

"And your hands." She lifted the one encroaching on personal territory and set it back on her waist, smiling with satisfaction. Lysett no longer held back in anything. Oh, he possessed her as thoroughly as all the times before, but he *talked* to her. With her. She could only share her perspective, but he valued her opinion and sought it. And she comforted him and supported him in turn. She doubted she could be more content.

"My hands want to take you upstairs." He tightened his hold, and the bar of his sex pressed against her belly. Duty and lust warred on his features, and then love softened them. "But you are tired. The babies take your energy."

The twins indeed took a lot out of her. The old healer had to eat crow—if there was such a bird on Meridia—when he retested her and determined another baby residing coyly behind the initial one he'd detected. He blamed missing it the first time on his excitement to find the royal concubine breeding.

The Ruler might not have been the first Meridian to conceive a child with an Earther, but Celeste was the only concubine carrying multiple fetuses—a boy and a girl. She ate constantly, now that food appealed, and indulged in naps so she could find the *energy* she wanted to expend, with Lysett.

"I have just enough for later," she teased and hid another smile when his eyes narrowed and he hardened further.

With a grimace, he adjusted his clothing and gestured around the room. "Then let us circulate and quickly make our excuses, Concubine."

Her body responded even more to the erotic

timbre of his voice, and she relished her title. His arm possessively around her, Lysett escorted her past Liaison Ashtun—Ash—and his blissfully happy Belinda, and several others. She nodded and smiled but in truth was so aware of the man she'd fallen in love with, she managed the barest acknowledgment. Not that they noticed, wrapped up in one another, much as she was with her Ruler.

"Come, Celeste." He steered her to the foot of the stairs, and gently propelled her upward.

"We're walking out on an important function." She tried to protest, as they left the noise of the gathering behind.

"No one here will even notice we're gone, and will probably be relieved to return to their homes and be alone with each other. As it should be." Taking her hand, he guided her up a step, then another, and rested his forehead against hers. "I love you, Celeste Raynor, Ruler's Concubine."

She fell into him, yet again, reveling in their intimacy. He would soon make her body sing, but these were the moments that sealed their connection. "And I love you, Lysett of the House of Daboort, Ruler of Meridia, and the Master of my heart."

The End

www.perielizabethscott.com

PERI ELIZABETH SCOTT

EVERNIGHT PUBLISHING ®

www.evernightpublishing.com